This book should be returned to any branch of the
Lancashire County Library on or before the date shown

1 1 APR 2017
1 2 MAY 2017   - 9 JAN 2019

1 4 JUL 2017

2 7 FEB 2018

2 0 JUN 2018

1 5 AUG 2018
- 2 OCT 2018

Lancashire County Library
Bowran Street
Preston PR1 2UX
www.lancashire.gov.uk/libraries

Lancashire
County
Council

LL1(A)

GREEK TYCOON'S
MISTLETOE
PROPOSAL

GREEK TYCOON'S MISTLETOE PROPOSAL

BY

KANDY SHEPHERD

HarperCollins
PUBLISHERS
Since 1817

First published in Great Britain 2016
By Mills & Boon, an imprint of HarperCollins*Publishers*
1 London Bridge Street, London, SE1 9GF

Large Print edition 2017

© 2016 Harlequin Books S.A.

Special thanks and acknowledgement go to Kandy Shepherd
for her contribution to the Maids Under the Mistletoe series.

ISBN: 978-0-263-07073-6

1

Printed and bound in Great Britain
by CPI Antony Rowe, Chippenham, Wiltshire

1191504027

To Wendy Uren—
for the many years of friendship and
all that window shopping in Bond Street!

CHAPTER ONE

LUKAS CHRISTOPHEDES HEARD the singing the moment he let himself into his Chelsea townhouse. The infernal sound of yet another Christmas carol. This time, infiltrating the sanctuary of one of his favourite homes. How many times had he heard a rendition of *Jingle Bells* already today? With only days until Christmas, canned festive music had followed him from the airport in Athens all the way to his disconcerting business meeting in east London. After the day he'd endured, he did *not* need *Jingle Bells* here.

The cleaner must have left a radio on. He had an ongoing arrangement with the upmarket Maids in Chelsea agency to ensure his house was cleaned and aired daily so it would always be ready should he have to spend time in the UK. Perhaps they'd purposely left the radio on as a burglar deterrent? That could make sense—Chelsea was one of the most affluent areas of London. But the sooner it was switched off the better.

As he strode through the marble-floored entranceway the singing got louder—and more off-key. He winced. No radio would give airtime to this appalling rendition of *Jingle Bells* in that tuneless female voice. This was a live performance. He cursed in a fluent mix of Greek and English. A maid must still be here working—a particularly tone-deaf maid. At six p.m. he expected his house to be free of any domestic help. It was his escape and his refuge and he demanded privacy. Strong words would be spoken to Maids in Chelsea for this breach of protocol.

Lukas flung his cashmere coat and scarf onto the antique chair in the marble-tiled hallway and headed towards the staircase that led to the next two floors. He wanted this maid out of his house, pronto.

The tuneless singing was coming from the next floor so he took the stairs two at a time. He wanted to plug his ears with his fingers as he neared the master bathroom that adjoined his bedroom. It couldn't be much fun getting down on hands and knees to scrub out someone's bathroom but that was no excuse for this tuneless wailing. The sooner this woman packed up her brushes and mops and got out, the better.

The door to the luxurious bathroom, all marble and glass, remodelled by one of the most in-demand interior designers in London, was half open. He pushed it fully open. Then stood, stupefied. *There was a naked woman in his bathtub.*

She reclined in the freestanding rolltop tub. Although a heavy froth of bubbles protected her modesty he could make out the shape of high, round breasts, slender shoulders, a long pale neck. A mass of bright auburn hair was piled on top of her head and fell in tendrils around a flushed heart-shaped face. One slim leg pointed to the ceiling as she used a long-handled wooden brush—*his* new brush—to soap between toes tipped with a delicate pink polish.

'*Oh, what fun it is to ride in a one-horse open sleigh-ay,*' she caterwauled, her voice cracking on the last word as she didn't achieve the high, extended note required.

Lukas stared in disbelief for a moment longer before he exploded. 'Who the hell are you and what are you doing in my bathroom?'

The woman turned. Her eyes widened and he saw they were an extraordinary shade of blue. Then she screamed—an ear-splitting scream even more excruciating to his ears than her singing. 'Get out!' she shrieked.

Lukas glared at her. 'You can get out of my bathtub first.'

She waved the bath brush at him in what was obviously intended to be a menacing manner. 'Not until you get out of here.'

The movement of wielding the brush brought her breasts dangerously close to being bared. With a quick downward glance and a little gasp, she seemed to realise it and stilled. Then slid deeper down into the water, all bravado wilting like the foam bubbles on her shoulders.

'I… I guess you're Mr Christophedes. Even though I was told you weren't going to be in London until after Christmas.'

'And *you* are?'

The flush deepened on her cheeks. 'Ashleigh Murphy. Your daily maid. From Maids in Chelsea.'

'So, Ashleigh Murphy, what are you doing in my bathtub?'

She raised the brush again. 'I'm…uh…scrubbing it.'

Her audacity almost made him smile. Almost. He realised she was young, mid-twenties at most. And quite lovely. But she had taken an unheard of liberty for a maid.

'I think not,' he said. He shifted his weight from foot to foot, crossed his arms in front of his chest. 'Try again.'

'This is such a luxurious bathroom. As I cleaned it, I wished I could try out the tub—it's magnificent, isn't it?' The hand that wasn't holding the bath brush reverently stroked the side of the tub without, Lukas thought, her realising she was doing it. 'The slum of a hotel where I've been staying has the world's most disgusting shared bathroom. I had to disinfect it before I could even think about dipping a toe in the tub. And then the water was just a lukewarm trickle…' Her voice died away. She swallowed hard. She didn't meet his eyes but seemed to concentrate on the work-of-art tap.

'So the bathroom is no better in the place you're staying now?'

She crinkled up her nose in a look that expressed guilt better than any words could. 'Actually it is. Because, well, I'm staying here. In… in your house.'

'You *what*?' The words exploded from him and she cringed back into the water.

'You're getting a live-in maid at no extra cost?' she offered, in an obvious effort to placate him.

'Not good enough, Ashleigh Murphy,' he thundered.

She crossed her arms over her chest and sat up higher in the bathtub. The water fell away to reveal more of her slim, pale body. Lukas knew he should avert his eyes but it wasn't easy. In his thirty-four years, he had never encountered such a situation. Even though he'd grown up in a multi-servant household and kept a full-time staff in his Athens mansion.

'I had nowhere else to stay. My time ran out at the hotel; I was planning to couch surf with a friend but it didn't work out. London at this time of year is so expensive I couldn't find anywhere I could afford. I'd been hired as your daily maid so I—'

'Took advantage and moved in.'

'Took advantage? I suppose that's how it might

look. But I was desperate. It was either bunk down in one of your guest rooms or…or go home.' Her voice trailed away.

'And home is?'

'Australia.'

He'd detected an accent but it wasn't strong and he hadn't been able to place it. Lukas frowned. 'Surely Australia is a good place to call home, especially at this time of year when it's summer there.'

Her eyes cast downward. 'Not…not when I ran away from my wedding. And if I go home again the family will think I've come back to… to marry a man I realised I don't love.'

She was a runaway bride? Lukas wasn't sure what to say about something so messy and to-tally out of his experience. But it was hardly an excuse to trespass. He cleared his throat. 'You'll be lucky if I don't call the police.'

Her eyes widened in alarm. 'Please. Don't do that. I assure you I haven't stolen anything. I've been doing extra cleaning in lieu of rent. And… and please don't tell Clio Caldwell at the agency,' she said. 'She knows nothing about me staying here. She's been so good to me and I don't want to let her down. And…and…well, she's having a personal crisis right now and doesn't need any extra worries.'

The fact that the intruder in his bathtub seemed more concerned at offending her boss than saving her own skin made Lukas soften towards her. Perhaps she was just young and silly, and desperate rather than dishonest.

'Then I suggest you pack your bags—'

'I only have a backpack,' she interrupted.

'Pack your *backpack* and get out of my house,' he said.

She caught her lower lip with her teeth. Lukas could not help noticing the lush fullness of her mouth, her perfect teeth. 'Now?' she said, her voice quivering a little on the word.

He tapped his foot on the floor. 'Now.'

'But…' Her voice trailed away and she hugged her arms closer to her chest.

Some dark part of him wanted to make her get out of the bath and watch as she fumbled for a towel. See for himself if her body was as slender and shapely as it appeared through the protective coating of bubbles. But he did not give in to base impulses. Not after having grown up with the consequences of his father's lack of self-control and indulgence in whatever appetites overcame him. Not when he'd been put at risk himself from the unbridled decadence of his family's lifestyle.

Lukas took a step towards the heated towel rail. Picked up a thick, pale grey towel and tossed it towards her. She went to catch it, her movement revealing the curve of the top of her breasts. Then, rather than risk further exposure, she stilled and let the towel slide to the marble tiles next to the tub. For a long moment she looked at him, her eyes wide, her mouth trembling. Lukas recognised the second a shadow of fear darkened her eyes as she realised the vulnerability of her position.

He stepped back to put a greater distance between them. He wanted her out of his house. But he would never want a woman to cringe from him in fear. Not that Ashleigh Murphy seemed to be the cringing type.

'Get yourself dressed and see me in my study on your way out,' he said curtly, turning on his heel. The sooner this opportunistic backpacker was out of his house the better.

* * *

Ashleigh towelled herself dry with trembling hands. Her encounter with Lukas Christophedes had left her shaking. Not just because she'd been caught trespassing by the owner of this multi-million-pound house but because of *him*. For that split second before she'd screamed, her senses had registered that the dark stranger in the bathroom was *gorgeous*.

As an Aussie girl from a country town, she had had no experience of Greek billionaires. If anything, she would assume they would be old, grey-haired and possibly paunchy—and there were no personal photos on display anywhere in this house to indicate Mr Christophedes was anything different.

The reality was that thirty-something Lukas Christophedes looked as if he'd stepped off the pages of an upmarket men's magazine—tall, broad-shouldered, dark-haired with a lean, handsome face. But his dark eyes had smouldered with fury, his mouth set tight when he'd discovered her in his bathtub. Gorgeous had suddenly seemed grim.

Thank heaven she didn't encounter him as she

made her way to the bedroom she'd purloined, wrapped only in the towel he had tossed at her. Of course she'd been completely in the wrong to have abused her position of trust with Maids in Chelsea to squat at a client's house. She'd been desperate but, in hindsight, she realised she must have been crazy to do such a thing.

As she dressed, then shoved her few belongings into her backpack, her mind roiled with thoughts of what she could say to him. If, as he'd threatened, he got the police involved, she could end up with a criminal record. Even get deported. And all because her friend Sophie had mysteriously disappeared on the night Ashleigh had intended to ask her if she could crash on her sofa until she found somewhere to live.

They'd been waitressing at a posh party and Ashleigh had been dealing with some obnoxious guests who'd downed rather too much champagne. By the time Ashleigh had sorted them, Sophie was nowhere to be seen—and hadn't reappeared until the next day with an enigmatic smile and a refusal to explain where she'd been.

In the meantime, Ashleigh had had nowhere to sleep. In desperation, she'd thought of the house in Chelsea where she'd just accepted a two-month house-care job. The luxury residence was empty and, apparently, rarely used.

It had been after midnight by the time Ashleigh had let herself into the Christophedes townhouse and the smallest of the guest rooms. With an en suite shower, it might actually be earmarked for a housekeeper or nanny she'd told herself to quieten her conscience. That first night she'd slept fitfully, fully clothed on top of the bedcover, jumping in panic at any slight sound in the house. By now, the third night, she'd convinced herself she wasn't hurting anyone and no one need know. Wasn't it a waste to leave a house like this empty? And she *had* made herself useful by doing chores beyond the scope of a daily maid's duties.

But, however much she'd tried to convince herself otherwise, she'd known staying there was wrong. What an idiot she'd been not to have just left it at one night. If she had, she might have got away with it. She dreaded facing Sophie, her friend she'd known since they were teenagers, who had recommended her for the position at Maids in Chelsea. Not to mention Clio. The charismatic owner of the agency had taken a risk on employing her—an unknown Australian with little prior experience of hospitality or house-keeping work.

Ashleigh slung her backpack over her shoulder. It was light. When she'd run away from her wedding, she'd only intended staying in London for a two-week vacation and had packed the minimum required. But she'd loved being in London so much she'd decided to quit her job back home and stay longer. Maids in Chelsea was hard work but fun and she'd made friends with two other maids as well as Sophie: posh Emma and shy Grace. She planned on staying in the UK for as long as it took to make it very clear to both Dan, her aggrieved former fiancé, and her family that she had no intention of returning home to get married. In her mind the ceremony was permanently cancelled. In their minds they seemed to think it had been merely postponed.

Sometimes it seemed her family sided more with Dan than with *her*. 'Dan is like a son to us, we're so fond of him,' her mother was always saying of the guy who had been Ashleigh's off and on boyfriend for years. Huh. That was the trouble. She'd realised she was *fond* of Dan too.

Just fond. Not the head-over-heels in love she needed to commit to marriage.

She'd explained that to her parents when she'd confessed she wanted to call off the wedding a month before she was due to walk down the aisle. In frustrated reaction to their shocked disbelief, she'd even gone so far as to call Dan *the world's most boring man.*

Instead of listening to her, instead of believing her, her mother had tut-tutted that she'd get over this little blip and that the stress of the wedding plans was messing with her mind. Her father had gone so far as to actually pat her on her head— as if she were seven instead of twenty-seven— and tell her there was nothing wrong with a bit of *boring* in a man. Boring meant steady and reliable. Ashleigh had gritted her teeth. Boring meant *boring.*

What did it take to get it into the heads of the folk back home that the engagement was *over*? She'd had every intention of going home to Bundaberg for Christmas. Her family celebrated Christmas in a big way and she'd never been away from them at this special time of year. But when the other day she'd video-chatted with her mother to talk about dates and flights, there was Dan, sitting beside her mum on the sofa. He'd blown her a kiss as if she still wore the engagement ring she'd consigned to the bottom drawer of her dressing table when he'd refused to take it back. *'You'll be wanting to wear it again,'* he'd said with pompous certainty.

Seeing him there, so complacent and cosy, had made her see red. It felt like a betrayal by her family. Then her mother had gushed that Dan would be with them for Christmas Day as both his mother and his father would be away. Without really thinking about the consequences, Ashleigh had informed her parents she was not coming home for Christmas and didn't know when she'd *ever* go back to Australia.

So here she was on a dark, freezing December evening, about to be booted out into the vastness of London without anywhere to stay. Except perhaps a police cell if she wasn't able to convince Lukas Christophedes to let her go.

She made her way up the stairs to the next level of the townhouse. There was an elevator, but she never took it, too frightened it might stall between floors and she'd be trapped in a house where she was staying illicitly. She sent up a prayer that the billionaire client would accept her grovelling apologies and let her go without punishment. Staying here had been a bad, bad idea.

She'd dusted and vacuumed around his already perfectly clean office so she knew where it was. Like all the rooms in this beautiful, luxurious house, it had been decorated with the most expensive of furnishings and fittings, yet still retained the cosiness of a traditional English library—the walls lined with books and Persian rugs on the floor.

The door was open. Lukas Christophedes sat at his desk, his back towards her. He'd taken off the jacket of his dark, superbly tailored business suit. The finely woven fabric of his shirt showed broad shoulders and a leanly muscled back. She knocked quietly and he immediately swivelled on his chair to face her.

She caught her breath, her trepidation momentarily overcome by heart-stopping awareness of his dark, Mediterranean good looks. He'd discarded his necktie and opened the top buttons of his shirt to reveal a vee of tanned olive skin pointing to an impressive chest. Rolled up sleeves showed strong, tanned forearms. His dark hair was rumpled as if he'd run it through with his fingers. For a moment, Ashleigh thought he seemed less intimidating. Until he turned his gaze to her, assessing her with narrowed eyes, his expression inscrutable.

A shiver travelled up her spine. This man had her in his power—and she had made herself vulnerable to him by her foolish behaviour. Talking her way out of this might not be easy.

CHAPTER TWO

LUKAS STARED AT Ashleigh Murphy as she peered around the door then stepped tentatively into his office. He schooled his face to hide his surprise. He'd been expecting a scruffy backpacker, the type travelling the world on a shoestring, seeking cut-price meals, free Wi-Fi and a cheap place to lay their heads. Backpackers of her ilk had filled the Greek seaside villages where he'd sailed and swam and partied as a student—before responsibility had grabbed him by the scruff and dragged him back to save the family business from his parents' gross mismanagement.

But Ashleigh Murphy seemed something more than that. True, she wore blue jeans that had seen better days, a sweater of some nondescript muddy colour and scuffed trainers. *Trainers.* His elegant mother would have hysterics at the sight of running shoes on the hand-woven carpet of a Christophedes residence. But there was something about this trespassing maid that transcended her humble attire and he found it difficult to drag his gaze away.

More petite than she'd appeared in his bathtub, fine-boned and slender, she moved with a natural grace. Her hair tumbled around her shoulders in a bright, untamed mass. It framed even features, pale skin flushed high on her cheekbones and those extraordinary blue eyes. Without even trying, she seemed *classy.*

He was still irritated by her outrageous incursion into his privacy. But Lukas's irritation began to dissipate as an idea began to form. An idea that could help him solve a particularly bothersome problem that, for all his business smarts, had him stumped. The problem had been plaguing him ever since his meeting at The Shard this afternoon. And it could impede the success of the business expansion he was determined to achieve.

But first he had to assess Ashleigh Murphy's suitability for what he had in mind. In the right clothes, her looks would pass muster. But he needed to find out more about her background, see if she was capable of what else was required.

Curtly, he indicated she take the chair on the other side of his desk. She put her backpack on the floor beside her and sat down. He made her wait while he tapped out some notations on his tablet. She sat up straight and appeared composed. Her attempt to mask her discomfort, perhaps even fear, at the situation in which she'd found herself was impressive. But she betrayed her anxiety in the way she shifted in her seat, her overly tight grip on the arms of the chair. In other circumstances, he would have put her at her ease. At this time, he felt it wouldn't hurt for her to squirm a little before he hit her with his demand.

He lifted his head to face her full on. 'I need to decide what course of action to take against the person I found basking in my bathtub instead of cleaning it.'

She flinched and the flush deepened on her cheekbones. 'Please, I can't apologise enough. I know how wrong it was to do what I did.' Her speaking voice, as opposed to her singing voice, was pleasant and well modulated.

'How long did you intend to stay here in my home?'

'Tonight. Then I—'

'You mean for as long as you could get away with it?'

'No!'

Lukas didn't reply. He'd learned silence often elicited more information than another question.

'Until I could find somewhere I could afford to live. I'm expecting a funds transfer from home any day. I... I haven't been working for Maids in Chelsea long enough to ask for an advance.'

She might not appear like the typical backpacker but it seemed she was as perpetually broke. That might play well into his hands.

'What kind of visa are you on that allows you to work in the UK?'

'No visa. My father is English by birth. I have an EU passport and the right of abode here.'

'Yet you live in Australia?'

'My grandparents emigrated when my father was a child. But we lived in Manchester for two years when I was a teenager while my father studied for his PhD.'

'Your father is an academic?'

'He's the principal of a secondary school in Bundaberg in Queensland where we live.'

'And your mother?'

'She's a schoolteacher too.' She tilted her head to one side in query. 'I don't know what that has to do with me doing the wrong thing here.'

'It interests me,' he said. *She* interested him.

She bit her lip, as if against a retort she wouldn't dare utter considering the precariousness of her situation.

'Have you always been a maid?'

'Of course not.' She spat out the words then backpedalled. 'Not that there's anything wrong with being a maid. In fact I consider myself to be a very good maid, and waitress and front-of-house person—all learned since I've been in London. But my real job is something quite different. I'm an accountant. I have a degree in commerce from the University of Queensland.'

'You—'

She put up her hand in a halt sign. 'Don't say it. If I had a dollar for every time someone told me I don't look like an accountant I'd be a wealthy woman.'

Lukas had to suppress a smile. That was exactly what he had been about to say. Of course there was no reason a woman so exquisitely feminine shouldn't be an accountant—it just made her even more interesting that she didn't fit the mould of an outmoded stereotype.

'You manage money for a living, yet you end up homeless in a big, ruthless city?' he said.

'Circumstances beyond my control,' she said, tight-lipped.

'Were you brought up by your family to be honest?'

Her eyes flashed with barely concealed outrage. 'Of course I was.'

'I could ask you to tip out the contents of your backpack for me to check, then to turn out your pockets.'

Her chin lifted. 'To see if I've stolen anything? I'd be more than happy for you to search my bag.' She gripped the arms of the chair and leaned forward. 'Go ahead. I have nothing to hide. But ask me to undergo a body search and it will be me calling the police.'

Lukas found he couldn't meet her fierce glare. He swallowed hard in distaste at his own actions. He had taken this too far. He had no desire to burrow through her personal belongings. Or undertake anything as intrusive as a body search. That would be…sleazy and he was not that kind of man. 'I'll take your word for it,' he said gruffly.

She nodded but her lips were pressed tight.

One of the reasons he'd been able to lift his family company from the verge of bankruptcy to a business turning over in the multiples of millions was his ability to read people. Every instinct told him this young woman had been foolish but not dishonest.

'I know Maids in Chelsea are scrupulous in the background checking of their employees,' he said. 'I assume the same was done for you.'

She rolled her eyes, just slightly, but he didn't miss it. It was an action he found unwarranted— but perhaps he would have done the same if he were on the other side of the desk.

'I can assure you I have no criminal record back in Australia,' she said. 'All I'm guilty of is an error of judgement. I know it was wrong of me and I reiterate my apology.'

'You admit you have slept under my roof. No doubt you were planning to spend tonight here too?'

'Yes. But it was only until—'

Lukas looked down at his tablet. 'I've calculated how much three nights at a West End hotel of equivalent comfort would cost you.' He named a figure that made her gasp. 'You owe me.'

Ms Murphy paled and he could see a sprinkling of freckles across the bridge of her nose. 'But I can't afford it. If I could pay that I would have gone to one of those hotels in the first place.'

He leaned back in his chair, steepled his fingers under his chin. 'That's really not my concern,' he said.

Lukas didn't like threatening her. But she could be a solution to his problem. And once he'd made up his mind on a course of action, he didn't stop until he'd got what he wanted.

'I... I can't,' she said. 'I just can't pay that.' Her lush, wide mouth trembled. 'You'd best call the police.'

Bravado or bravery? Whatever it was, he admired her spirit.

He narrowed his eyes. 'There's no need for me to call the police. I have a way you can pay off your debt to me without money exchanging hands. Something not very arduous that you might even enjoy.'

* * *

Ashleigh was up and out of her chair so fast she tripped on her backpack and had to steady herself against the desk. She could hardly believe what she'd heard. Sexual favours to pay off a so-called fabricated debt? Clio had warned her there was a certain type of man who considered maids and waitresses to be fair game. Already she'd had to fend them off—especially towards the end of the night at a party when they'd had too much to drink. But *this* man! She was shocked—and disappointed. Lukas Christophedes had seemed better than that.

'No,' she said. 'Never.'

He frowned, got up from his chair. The man was tall and powerfully built and she was glad there was a desk between them. 'You say "no" before you've even heard my proposition?' he asked, his frown deepening.

'Sex is sex, no matter which variant you want me to trade with you.' She glared at him then glanced at the open door, ready to bolt. 'And the answer will always be no.'

He frowned. 'You've got this wrong. I didn't mean that at all.' He wiped his hand across his forehead. 'I would never suggest such a thing. My English...'

His lightly accented English was perfect. It wasn't *what* he'd said but *how* he'd said it. Then she took in the bewilderment in his deep brown eyes and swallowed hard. Or could it be how *she'd* interpreted his words?

'Maybe I...misunderstood?' she asked hesitantly. Misunderstood big time, perhaps.

He came around the desk towards her. She took a step away, the back of her knees pressed against the edge of the chair. Just in case. After all, he was a stranger and she was alone with him in his house.

'Whether I did not get my message across correctly or you misunderstood is beside the point,' he said. 'I am not asking you for *sex*. That is not how I do business.'

'I... I'm glad to hear it.' He must think her hopelessly naïve. 'So...what is your proposition?'

'I want you to pretend to be my girlfriend.'

Ashleigh felt as though all the air had been expelled from her lungs. 'You *what*! How is that different from—'

He put up one large, well-shaped hand to halt

her flow of words. 'Completely above board, I assure you. Just for one evening. An important business dinner tomorrow. I've decided I need a date to…to deflect unwanted interest.'

'And you want me to be a fake date?'

'Exactly.'

'Why? I can't imagine a man like you would have a shortage of real dates. You're wealthy, handsome. You'd just have to click your fingers for a multitude of women to come running.'

'Perhaps not a multitude.' He gave a wry, self-deprecating smile she found herself warming to. 'Of course I know a few women in London.' Ashleigh suspected that was a serious understatement. 'But none whom I want to involve in this. No one I want to get the wrong impression.'

'You mean the impression you're serious about her.'

'That is correct,' he said. 'This would be purely a business deal, with no continuing personal involvement. You are unknown in London and that suits me perfectly.'

Would being this man's fake date be any worse than being hired as a waitress for an upscale private party? The idea intrigued her. *He* intrigued her. Wasn't this why she'd come to London? To climb out of the deep rut she'd found herself in. To revel in freedom and independence. To be brave and take risks and open up to new experiences.

'So tell me more about this "proposition"?' she said.

Ashleigh stood by the chair close to her backpack, on the off chance she needed to pick it up and run. He paced up and down as he spoke.

'I met this afternoon at The Shard with a potential business partner, someone I very much want to work with.'

Ashleigh loved the beautiful old buildings in London where history was alive on every corner. But she was fascinated by The Shard—London's futuristic glass skyscraper. The first day she'd arrived, she'd stood at its base and craned her neck to gaze up at the incredible ninety-five-storey building, so tall its jagged top disappeared into the clouds. One rare free evening when they weren't working, she and Sophie had gone up to the bar for a drink—just one as they were so expensive—and gawked at the incredible views of London old and new.

Of course The Shard would be just the place for a visiting billionaire to hold his meetings.

'Excuse my ignorance,' Ashleigh said. 'But what exactly is your business?'

There was no point in pretending she knew anything about him—or in pretending she was anything other than who she was. Of course, if she agreed to be his fake date, that would take pretending to a whole new level. *He was so handsome it wouldn't be a hardship.*

'There are various arms to the Christophedes business but the one that concerns me now is electrical appliances. We dominate the Greek market, are one of the bestselling brands in mainland Europe, and export to Scandinavia and the Middle East. But the British market eludes me. I need a local partner.'

'You mean a distributor?'

'Yes. I did my due diligence and decided this woman's company would be the best fit for what I need. I approached her and today was our initial meeting.'

'Is she interested in doing business with you?'

'Yes.' He stopped his pacing, looked directly down at her. 'She is also interested in me.'

'That's good, isn't it?' she said, perplexed at the doom-laden way he said it. 'You would have to get on with her if you're working on such a big deal.'

He cleared his throat and shifted from foot to foot. Ashleigh was surprised at his display of discomfort. 'I mean she is interested in me as not just a business partner but as a man.'

For the first time Ashleigh saw a crack in the billionaire's confident air of arrogance. She tried not to smile. Somehow she doubted that was the reaction he would expect. 'I see,' she said, trying to sound very serious.

'Do you? Tina Norris is a very beautiful older woman used to getting her own way.'

'So…she's a cougar and she wants you as part of the deal?' Who could blame the woman? The man was good-looking in the extreme. And, she suspected, when he wasn't glaring or shouting at misbehaving maids, he could be charming.

'That is the impression she gave me this afternoon.' He shuddered. Again Ashleigh had to suppress a smile. He was no doubt used to being the hunter, not the hunted.

'But you're not interested?'

'Not in the slightest. I found her...predatory. Besides, I would never get involved with a business partner.'

'I see your dilemma—you don't want to offend her.'

'That is correct. I want her on side for the business.'

'But not in your bed.'

He paused. 'That's a blunt way of putting it, but yes.'

'Hence the fake date. It would be diplomatic if she could see you had a girlfriend.'

'Exactly,' he said.

'But you don't want to give the wrong idea to someone you might actually date.' Ashleigh felt she had to reiterate to make sure she completely understood what she might or might not be getting herself into. She was surprised at how at ease she felt with him.

'Yes.'

'And that's where I come in? If I agree, that is. What would my—' she used her fingers to make quotation marks '—*duties* involve?'

'Accompany me for the evening. Make intelligent conversation—I can see that won't be a problem—and behave as though we are a genuine couple. Convince Ms Norris that there is no point in pursuing me as I am already involved with a beautiful redhead.' He looked at her with what seemed like genuine admiration. She couldn't help but preen a little.

'So, act all lovey-dovey?'

'I'm not exactly sure what you mean by that but I think I get the gist of it,' he said with that ghost of a smile she was beginning to anticipate.

'You know, act affectionate and smoochy with each other.' *Why had she said that?* Because she realised that if she had met this man in different circumstances she would find the idea of smooching with him more than a touch appealing.

'It will be a business dinner,' he said. 'Anything…physical would have to be discreet.'

'I get it,' she said. Ashleigh wondered if he was subtly warning *her* not to form any expectations of anything other than a fake date with him.

He stood with his back to the window, his hands clasped behind him. The curtains were drawn against the cold of a December evening, but she knew the window looked down to a city-sized garden, perfectly maintained with formal clipped hedges and a centrepiece fountain. No doubt there was a team of gardeners to keep it in shape for when the absentee owner decided to drop into London.

She looked up at him, wishing she wasn't wearing flat shoes—he was so much taller than her and his superior height seemed to emphasise the balance of power that tipped firmly in his favour. The billionaire and the maid.

'If I agreed to your proposition, what would be the consequences for me?' she asked.

'No complaint would be made against you to your employer or the police.'

'And my "debt" to you?' That calculation of hotel rates rankled. She doubted he would be able to enforce something so spurious. But she was hardly in a position to question his methods. Not when he had every right to report her to the police.

'Of course your debt would be wiped completely.'

'In return for one dinner date with you and your potential business partner?'

'Yes,' he said.

Ashleigh didn't ask if she would continue to be his daily maid. She knew she'd flicked her last ever duster around this house. She'd have to invent a good excuse to give Clio for why she wanted to quit such a pleasant job.

'It sounds like it could be fun,' she said, forcing a smile. What choice did she have but to agree?

'As I said, you might even enjoy it,' he said. 'The dinner is at an excellent restaurant in Mayfair.' The kind of place maids usually didn't eat at was the implication. Or indeed accountants from Bundaberg.

She took a deep breath. 'Okay, I'll do it,' she said. 'But there's just one more thing.'

He raised a dark eyebrow. 'Yes?'

'How will we get around the fact that we're total strangers and know absolutely nothing about each other?'

CHAPTER THREE

'HOW DO WE get over the hurdle that we are strangers? We start finding out about each other,' Lukas said. 'We have until tomorrow evening to make our story sound feasible.'

He was pleased Ashleigh had acquiesced so readily. So he'd had to use some leverage to get her on board, but that was what it took sometimes to get a deal across the line. He'd learned that at twenty-one when he'd had to sort out the mess his profligate parents had made of the company. It had been a tough lesson—he'd discovered people he'd thought he could trust could not be trusted, that he had to be guarded, tamp down on his reactions and feelings. The episode had marked the end of his youth.

'You mean I get a crash course in Greek billionaire and you learn what makes an Aussie maid tick?' she said.

'Aren't you masquerading as a maid? That's just

a vacation job, isn't it? I suggest you stick to Aussie accountant,' he said. 'We'll skirt around the maid thing as far as Tina Norris is concerned.' No doubt Ms Norris would have done her research, discovered he was a steadfast bachelor, would scrutinise the woman he chose to accompany him. He shuddered again at the thought of the predatory gleam in the older woman's eye when they'd met. Buried in his past was good reason for his revulsion.

'Actually, I don't much like being an accountant,' Ashleigh said. 'I was steered into it by my parents, who thought accountancy would bring a secure job. I've got my options wide open when it comes to changing career.'

'You'll need to brief me on all that,' he said.

The briefing would not be onerous—there was something about this girl that intrigued him. Ashleigh Murphy seemed somehow different to the women he usually met. Perhaps because she was Australian. More likely because she didn't move in the same social circles. He liked that she didn't seem intimidated by him or fall over backwards to impress him.

She shrugged. 'Not much to tell, really. I managed a flooring company back home.'

'You were a manager? That's impressive.' She didn't appear to be long out of university.

Her slight smile in response hinted at dimples and he found himself wanting to make her smile properly. Not that he was adept at telling jokes or funny stories. In fact he'd been accused of being over-serious. Since he'd been forced to swap his carefree life as a wealthy kid who'd known he would never have to work for a living, there had been little room for laughter. Or for love.

Where did that come from? Perhaps prompted by the knowledge that, at the age of thirty-four, he had to *pretend* he had a serious woman in his life. A wife, children—there wasn't room in his life for marriage. *He didn't want all that.* And, he told himself, he didn't miss it. The Christophedes companies took up all his life. The business *was* his life.

'The title sounds more impressive than it is,' she said. 'It's a small company and I wore a few different hats. But it had a good product and I worked with really nice people. Truth is, you can't be too picky when it comes to getting a good job in a country town. There aren't many opportunities.'

Lukas couldn't imagine why a woman as smart and lovely as Ashleigh Murphy would want to bury herself in some far-flung country town. He would find out why tonight.

He glanced at his watch. 'Have you eaten?'

'No. I was…er…going to have something after my bath.'

'So you've been using my kitchen too?'

She nodded. 'I won't lie,' she said. 'Though it sounds like I might be doing a lot of lying tomorrow night.'

'Not *lying*.' He refused to contemplate that he was planning anything that smacked of dishonesty. 'Think of it as role playing.'

Her auburn eyebrows rose. 'Not a bad idea. I've done some acting—amateur, of course— so I'll think of this as preparing for a role.' She pulled a face. 'You might have to help me with the script.'

'Starting from now,' he said. They had until tomorrow, but a good part of his day would be, as usual, taken up with work. 'You haven't eaten

and I haven't eaten. Come out to dinner with me
and we'll start the get-to-know-you process.'

'Uh, okay,' she said, obviously disconcerted.
'But…but I need to find somewhere to stay tonight. I have to phone around my friends.' She
looked at her feet, obviously uncomfortable at
the reminder of her transgression. As well she
might be.

'You can stay here tonight,' he said.

She looked up. 'As part of the deal?'

'Yes,' he said. Whatever she might think of
him, he would not let a young woman risk being
alone in London without a safe place to sleep.
'Though you can steer clear of my bathroom.'

'And what about tomorrow night?' she said, audacity trickling back into her demeanour.

'Tomorrow night too.'

For the first time since he had encountered her
in his bathtub Ashleigh smiled. Delightful dimples bracketed her cheeks and light danced in her
eyes. He found himself dazzled by the warmth
and vivacity that smile brought to her face. She
really was lovely, in a wholesome, unsophisticated way.

'Thank you,' she said again. 'That will give

me the breathing space I need to make other arrangements.'

'After that you'll be on your own,' he cautioned her.

'I'm aware of that,' she said. 'I realise I'm only here on sufferance.' She paused. 'Just checking I won't be charged accommodation fees for those two extra nights?'

'Of course not,' he said, an edge of impatience burring his voice. 'You're now an invited guest.'

'Just needed to be sure,' she said, but there was an impish gleam to her eyes that made him unsure if she was completely serious. He wasn't used to being teased.

He looked pointedly at his watch. 'I suggest you go back downstairs and change.'

She looked down at her jeans and trainers, as if seeing them for the first time. 'Yes, these clothes won't do, will they? I'm warning you, though, I don't have the wardrobe to be a billionaire's escort.' She flushed. 'I mean "escort" in the old-fashioned sense of the word, not… uh…the other.'

'I thought I'd made it very clear that this is strictly business.' Now he felt like rolling his eyes.

'Yes, you did,' she said. 'And I didn't mean...' Her words petered to a halt. She walked back to the desk and picked up her backpack. 'I'll go down to change now. Shall I meet you at the bottom of the stairs in ten minutes?'

He nodded, secretly sceptical about the ten minutes. Never had he known a woman to get ready for a dinner date in that small amount of time.

She headed towards the door. Again, he thought how gracefully she moved. It made watching her do something as simple as walk away a pleasure. But she stopped and turned on her heel to face him again. 'Mr Christophedes, before I go, I want to thank you for...well, for being so reasonable about all this. I appreciate it and I want to assure you that in return I'll do my very best for you with the fake date scenario.'

It gave him a jolt that she called him *Mr Christophedes*. The formal usage felt as if she had put him in his place—an older guy, an employer, someone of a different generation to be kept at a distance.

He didn't know why he didn't like it. But she couldn't keep calling him Mr Christophedes when they were together with Tina Norris. That would give away the game.

Ashleigh didn't wait for an answer and her quickened pace as she left the room made it clear she didn't expect one.

Lukas looked at the doorway for a long moment after she'd left. Who would have thought the maid in his bathtub would turn out to be such an interesting woman?

Ten minutes later, he was amazed to find Ashleigh waiting for him at the base of the staircase. She'd used the time to advantage. He was so taken aback by the result he was momentarily lost for words. Once again, she'd surprised him.

No trace of backpacker remained. She wore a simple black dress, buttoned down the front and belted at the waist, with elbow-length sleeves. The hem stopped just above her knees to display slender legs encased in fine charcoal stockings and finished with low-heeled black pumps.

'Do I look okay for the restaurant?' she said, aware of his overly long inspection.

Her hair had been tamed and pulled half back off her face. She'd darkened around her eyes, which made them look even bluer, and her mouth gleamed with a warm pink lipstick.

'You look very nice,' he said, then cursed inwardly that he'd used such an overworked English word. *Eisai omorfi* were the words that sprang to his mind—*You look beautiful.* But that would be inappropriate.

'Great, because this is the only dress I've got with me,' she said with a sigh of relief. 'It's what I wear when I'm waitressing at posh parties. Maids in Chelsea doesn't have a uniform—a black dress is required for such occasions. My friend Sophie gave this to me when I started there. She's a fashion designer—when she's not a maid or waitress, that is—she'd made it for herself then adjusted it to fit me.' She smiled. 'But I guess that's too much information, isn't it?'

Lukas was still shaken by his reaction to how good she looked in that dress. It was discreet, modest even, but it fitted snugly and made no secret of her curves, a hint of cleavage in the open neckline, the belt emphasising her narrow waist and the flare of her hips. He had to clear his voice to speak. 'Not really. Now I know you have a friend Sophie who is generous and good to you.'

Ashleigh smiled—not her full-on dazzling smile but halfway to it. 'I went to school in Manchester with Sophie when we were teenagers and we've always stayed in touch. She got me the job too. Then introduced me to two of the other girls at Maids in Chelsea and we've all become friends.' She looked up at him, that smile still hovering around her mouth. 'But none with a sofa available when I needed it.'

Lukas smiled in response. He wouldn't go so far as to say he was glad she'd ended up at his house—but his outrage at her impudence had dissipated.

'You'll be cold when we get outside.' He noticed she had a coat slung over her arm. 'Get your coat on and we'll walk to the restaurant.'

She shrugged on her coat and once again Lukas stared at her, this time in what he feared was ill-concealed dismay. Of course she picked up on it. 'It's not great, is it?' she said of the shabby quilted anorak that didn't meet the hem of her dress.

'Is that the only coat you have?'

'A warm overcoat is not something you need

in Bundaberg's tropical climate,' she said. 'I borrowed this from my sister from when she backpacked around Europe. I'm waiting until next payday to buy something more suitable for London.'

'In the meantime, you shiver?' he said.

'Let's just say I walk really fast when I'm outside,' she said. 'Oh, and these help.' From out of her coat pocket she pulled a hideous checked scarf and a pair of knitted mittens and flourished them in front of him. Lukas had to refrain from shuddering his distaste. He might have his issues with his mother but she was the most elegantly dressed woman he knew, and had set the standard for how he expected a woman to dress. He'd have to schedule a shopping expedition for Ashleigh in the morning so she looked the part for their fake date.

'You can't wear that out with me,' he said, too bluntly.

'Oh,' she said, suddenly subdued. Without protest, she slid the odious excuse for a coat off her shoulders. 'Then I guess I'll shiver in just my dress.' With great exaggeration, she wrapped her arms around herself and made her teeth chatter. 'I'll walk really, *really* fast to the restaurant.'

'No need for that,' he said, heading for the cloakroom under the stairs. 'My mother left a coat behind on her last visit. She's a little taller than you but I think it will fit.'

'Your mother won't mind?'

'My mother has so many clothes she's probably forgotten she has it,' he said.

Lukas flicked through the coats and jackets he left here for his own use. 'Here it is,' he said and pulled out a wraparound coat of fine wool in a subtle leopard print with a shawl collar. A faint whiff of his mother's signature perfume drifted to his nostrils. It brought memories of his glamorous mama kissing him goodnight before she headed out for yet another party, leaving him once again with his nanny. He'd grown up loving his nanny more than his mother. He held out the coat to Ashleigh.

'Oh, I *love* it,' she breathed, her eyes wide with admiration. 'Are you sure it's okay for me to wear it?'

'Would I offer if it wasn't?'

'It's just that it looks very expensive.'

'I'm sure it is,' he said. His mother's extravagance wasn't the sole reason his parents' management of the company had brought the business crashing to its knees, but it had certainly contributed to it.

He held the coat open. 'Here, let me help you into it.'

As Ashleigh slid her arms into the coat it brought her close to him. So close he could smell *her* scent—something fresh and light and appealing. Much like Ashleigh herself.

She shrugged the coat over her shoulders, headed to the large mirror on the wall opposite the stairs. There she tied the belt around her waist, adjusted the collar. Then fluffed up her hair and pouted at her image as she scrutinised her appearance, in a gesture that was instinctively feminine. She snuggled into the coat and closed her eyes in bliss. Lukas was stunned by the sensuality of her expression he saw reflected in the mirror.

'This is the most wonderful coat,' she purred as she stepped away from the mirror. 'I've never worn anything like it. Thank you, Mrs Christophedes.' She blew a kiss in the direction of the cloakroom. The warm tones of the leopard print were perfect for her colouring, making her hair seem to flame under the hallway chandelier, lifting her pale skin. She did a graceful little twirl and the hem of the coat swung open to show her legs. *She looked sensational.* 'And thank you too, *Mr* Christo—'

'Lukas,' he said gruffly, keeping his hands fisted by his sides.

'Of course,' she said. *'Lukas.'* His name sounded like a caress on her voice. 'I'll have to get used to calling you that. Be careful not to give the game away when we're on our fake date.'

'Yes,' he said.

He would have to be careful too. When he'd devised the solution to the problem with Tina Norris, he hadn't expected to feel any stirrings of attraction to his pretend girlfriend. *He could not let that happen.*

'You know, *Lukas*,' she said, exaggerating his name. 'You were right. I think I really am going to enjoy this…role playing.' She unleashed the full force of her dazzling smile. 'Let's get started straight away.'

CHAPTER FOUR

ASHLEIGH STOOD NEAR the top of the marble steps that led to the street, stamping her feet in her thin-soled pumps against the cold. It seemed surreal to be on her way out to dinner with Lukas Christophedes—billionaire, businessman, *fake boyfriend.*

As she well knew, it took time to attend to the various locks, bolts and security devices on the glossy black front door. She seized those few minutes to herself to try and sort her chaotic thoughts about the crazy deal she'd struck with him.

But as she watched him she started to shiver—not because of the cold but from delayed reaction as the full impact of her misconduct hit her. Security was vital to the high-end clients of Maids in Chelsea. She'd learned that London SW3 was one of the most desirable postcodes in the UK, possibly even the world. By handing her the keys to this house, Clio had entrusted her with the reputation of the agency—and she had betrayed that trust big time.

She felt she might hyperventilate when she realised how lucky she was to have got off so lightly. Had anyone other than Lukas Christophedes caught her in his bathtub she suspected she would right now be languishing in a police lockup. But his lenient treatment of her was only because she had something to offer him. If he changed his mind, or if she didn't deliver on her part of the bargain, she could still end up enjoying the hospitality of the Kensington and Chelsea constabulary.

Men like Lukas—no matter how charming— didn't get to be billionaires without being ruthless. She would have to play her assigned role to the nines. That meant getting as much as she could out of this evening so she could become the best pretend girlfriend ever. Then, after tomorrow's dinner date was over, she could put him and today's mortifying incident behind her. She took a deep breath to steady herself for the task to come.

Not that spending time with Lukas would exactly be a hardship. As he finished with the security device he turned to face her. Tall and imposing in a superbly tailored, deep charcoal overcoat, he was so strikingly handsome if she'd passed him in the street she would probably have tripped over her feet in her haste to turn and gawk at him. He was intelligent and interesting too. It seemed impossible that such a gorgeous man had to resort to a fake date. One thing was for sure—she could never think of Lukas Christophedes as *boring*.

He narrowed his eyes in the inscrutable way she had already come to recognise. 'You need boots in this weather,' he said. 'Tall black boots.'

She stopped stamping, berating herself for drawing attention to the paucity of her wardrobe. 'Yes,' she said. If he only knew how many of London's enticing shop windows she had lingered at, looking at boots she couldn't possibly afford. Running away from her wedding had cost her in more ways than one. 'Warm boots are on my shopping list.' To be purchased at the Christmas sales. She had to find somewhere to live first, before she bought boots.

He indicated that she go ahead of him down the steps. 'Do you like Italian food?' he asked.

Her tummy threatened to rumble in response. She hastened to speak over it. 'I like any food. Well, pretty well any food. I don't care too much for really hot curries, which is a disadvantage living in London when that's what my friends love best. But Italian? I love Italian. Wouldn't you like to eat Greek?'

'No one cooks Greek food as well as in Greece,' he said, his voice underscored with arrogance.

'I guess not. I've enjoyed Greek food back home in Australia,' she said. 'You know Melbourne is supposed to have the biggest population of Greek people of any city outside of Greece? Not that I'd recognise what was good Greek food or bad.'

Ashleigh knew she was chattering on too much, a habit she would have to curb if she were to be believable as the sophisticated kind of woman a man like this would date. *Lukas and her.* She had to get the script right. Because this might very well turn out to be one of the most life-changing experiences of her life.

'I'll take you to my favourite Italian restaurant on the King's Road,' he said.

'I'd like that,' she said.

As soon as she turned into the street, she gasped as a gust of cold, damp air hit her, burning her lungs, numbing her cheeks. Her eyes started to water and she blinked against the smarting tears.

'You're not used to the cold, are you?' Lukas asked.

'Not yet,' she said, rubbing her hands together then sliding them into the pockets of her glorious borrowed coat. 'I'm still getting acclimatised. Of course I spent very cold, wet winters in Manchester when I was younger but that was years ago. I've lived in tropical heat ever since.'

Immediately, Lukas unwound the finely woven grey scarf from around his neck. 'Wear this and keep it up around near your face.'

Dumbfounded, Ashleigh shook her head. 'There's no need—I can't possibly take your scarf.' It was all very well to wear his mother's clothing; to wear *his* clothes seemed way too intimate.

Did he intend to put it around her neck? She put up her hand to stop him and in doing so grazed his. At the brief contact, she dropped her hand—then regretted it immediately. A pretend girlfriend wouldn't react like that at such a casual touch. A pretend girlfriend *certainly* shouldn't feel such a zing of awareness.

'But you must,' he said, holding the scarf out to her. 'I insist.' It was not so much a demand but a statement not to be disputed.

Pretend girlfriend or not, it would be ungracious not to take the scarf when it had been so thoughtfully offered. Tentatively, she took it from him. The fabric was soft, cashmere and silk most likely, and warm from his body heat. She wound it around her neck, tucked it inside her collar and up around her chin, and immediately felt several degrees cosier.

'Thank you,' she said simply, too shaken to say anything else.

The scarf was scented with something spicy and woody—cedar perhaps?—and distinctly male. *Him.* The scent of Lukas Christophedes—the man she needed to get to know by this time tomorrow evening. The man she would have to fight crazy stirrings of attraction for. There was too much of a fairy tale feel about all this—she couldn't allow herself to believe any of it could be real.

'But now you'll be cold without your scarf,' she said.

'I'll have to walk really, *really* fast then,' he said, taking an exaggerated deeper stride.

She laughed, surprised at the unexpected touch of humour. Otherwise he seemed so *serious.*

'Does it get cold in Greece in winter?' she asked. 'I always think of it as a summer place, all blue skies and even bluer waters.'

'Even the islands get snow in winter,' he said. 'I live in Athens where it does get cold but not bitterly so. Then we have unexpected warm days— *halkionis meres*—halcyon days when the sun is shining and winter is temporarily banished.'

They were talking about the weather. She'd need to know more than that if she were to fool the astute businesswoman they'd be dining with tomorrow. But where to start without seeming to interrogate him?

They walked to the end of his street, turned into The Vale and then right into the King's Road, heading west. Far from walking really, really fast, Lukas kept his pace to hers. *As if they actually were a couple.* At this time of evening Chelsea was buzzing. Trees were strung with thousands of tiny lights, the shops decorated for Christmas, snatches of festive music greeting them as they walked by the buildings. London at Christmastime was magic—she was so glad she had decided to stay here.

'Where shall we say we met?' she asked, having to raise her voice over the sound of a red number eleven bus rumbling by. 'We can't say Greece, because I've never been to your country. I did a whistle-stop European bus tour when I was a student but we didn't go there.'

'We'll rule out Greece, then. I believe my potential business partner has vacationed on the island of Santorini many times and would immediately sniff out any fraud.'

'Have you ever been to Australia?' she asked.

'No. Although it is on my bucket list.'

'So "no" to Australia, then. Seems our common ground is England. We'll have to say we met somewhere on British soil.'

'But not in my bathroom.'

Was there a hint of teasing in his expression? Ashleigh couldn't see to be sure. She squirmed at the memory of their first meeting. 'No,' she said. 'Definitely not.' Maybe she would tell Sophie about that incident but no one else. She would never live it down.

'When were you in Manchester?' Lukas asked.

'When I was fifteen. Twelve years ago. And Sophie tells me the city has changed a lot.'

'Manchester won't work either.' He paused. 'So you're twenty-seven now?'

'You sound surprised.'

'I thought you were younger. Perhaps twenty-three, twenty-four.'

Ashleigh gritted her teeth. She couldn't let him know how much that assumption irritated her. 'People often take me for younger—and treat me as younger.' Especially her family—right now refusing to believe she knew how she wanted to live her own life. 'I'll be twenty-eight in March and am quite grown up, thank you.' She couldn't keep the tart edge from her words.

'I'll keep that in mind,' he said with that trace of a smile that lifted his somewhat severe face.

'How old are you?' she asked. If there'd been time, she would have looked him up on the Internet. As it was, she was flying blind. *He was a total stranger.*

'Thirty-four.'

'So you were okay with thinking I was more than ten years younger than you?'

'In my family it is not uncommon for the men to be much older than their women. My father is considerably older than my mother.'

'I see,' she said. She'd only ever dated men around her own age. It might be interesting to get to know a man six years older—even if they weren't *really* dating. 'There's so much I need to know about you if we're to appear authentic as a couple.'

'That is true. Ask me anything you need to know.'

'And you ask me anything too,' she said. Not that there was a lot to discover. Her life had been anything but exciting. *Until now.*

They walked in silence while Ashleigh wrote herself a mental memo of questions. She fired off the one at the top of her list. 'I probably don't need to ask this, but I'm assuming you're not married?'

'I have never been married,' he said. 'I never will marry.'

His vehemence surprised her. 'That answers that, then,' she said. 'I'm…uh…sure you have your reasons.' He didn't rush to enlighten her as to those reasons. 'What about serious girlfriends?'

'Not recently. And none that should concern you.'

'Not married. No serious girlfriends. Okay.' *This wasn't going well.*

'My friends tell me I'm married to my work.'

'Really? That doesn't sound much fun.'

His laugh was short and cynical. 'One thing you would be expected to know about me is that I took over the family business when it was on the verge of bankruptcy. I was aged twenty-one when I set myself the goal of turning it around. There hasn't been much opportunity for *fun*.'

'That's quite a story. You must be proud of such an achievement.'

'Yes,' he said shortly.

'But what's the point of being a billionaire and not having any fun?'

Lukas stopped so abruptly she nearly crashed into him. *'What?'* he said.

'I said… I said… Well, I think you heard what I said. I mean, life's all about laughter and love and…' Her voice dwindled away. 'Forget it. On to the next question.'

He stared at her in what she could only describe as astonishment that she should be so impertinent. 'My life is about responsibility and hard work and righting the wrongs of the past,' he said.

She didn't dare ask what those wrongs might be. Not yet, anyway.

'I get that,' she said, even though she didn't. *They came from different worlds.* She forced her voice to sound bright and cheerful. *What the heck had she got herself into?*

'Moving on to my next question. You speak such perfect English. Did you study here?' His voice was deep and steady, with that hint of an accent to add to its appeal. She could close her eyes and just enjoy hearing him talk.

'I went to university here in London for a while. But I was already fluent. I had an English nanny from birth and studied the language all through school. My family considered it important that I spoke good English. There is another reason so many young Greek people speak English— American and English music and movies are not often dubbed into Greek.'

'That's a powerful incentive to learn a language. I wish I'd had something like that to inspire me.'

'Do you speak another language?'

'I studied Indonesian at school. But, apart from vacations in Bali, I've never really used the language so am not at all fluent.' She looked up at him. 'Maybe you can teach me some Greek?'

'There is not much I can teach you in the short time we will be together,' he said. *Putting her in her place.*

'Of course,' she said. 'But could you please just tell me the Greek for "darling"?'

He frowned. 'What for?'

She wanted to sigh heavily at his obtuseness but didn't dare. Wasn't it obvious? 'An endearment here and there might add to the authenticity of our…uh…relationship.'

'Agápi mou,' he said finally.

'I beg your pardon?'

'It means *darling*, or *my love—agápi mou*,' he said with an edge of impatience.

Ashleigh repeated the words. 'How did I do?' she asked.

'Not bad at all,' he said with an expressive lifting of his dark eyebrows.

'Thank you.' In her head she went over and over the phrase so it would seem natural should she get the chance to drop it into the conversation.

They walked further, past the fashionable restaurant that had in some earlier incarnation been a garage. She'd enjoyed a very expensive cup of coffee there with Sophie the first day she'd come to Chelsea to meet Clio and be interviewed for the position with the agency.

'How far is the restaurant?' she asked.

'A few blocks further down,' he said.

'Towards Land's End?'

He smiled. 'World's End is in Chelsea. Land's End is in Cornwall, right down at the southern-most part of England. They say if you walk from John O'Groats at the top of Scotland to Land's End you've walked the length of Britain.'

Ashleigh gave herself a mental slam to the

forehead. 'Of course, what a stupid mistake. I've heard my English grandparents say that. You know more about this country than I do and I've got English blood.'

'I like London. That's why I bought the house here. Chelsea is so English but also cosmopolitan. I can enjoy a certain anonymity here.'

'I love it too,' Ashleigh said. She was about to tell him how she'd felt immediately at home in London when she'd got here but didn't want to remind him of how completely she'd made herself at home in his house.

The *ristorante* was large and noisy with clatter and chatter; delicious aromas wafted to meet her. Ashleigh wondered how she would be able to talk privately with Lukas. But he was greeted by name by the beaming *maître d'* who took their coats—she hoped hers wouldn't get lost because no way in a million years would she ever be able to afford to replace it—and ushered them to a quiet table in an alcove. Reluctantly, she handed over her borrowed scarf—already she missed its warm caress with the heady hint of his scent.

The waiter pulled out her chair for her. But before she sat down she rose up on tiptoe and deliberately planted a lingering kiss on Lukas's cheek, then trailed her fingers from his cheek, down his neck to stop at his collar. 'This is delightful, *agápi mou,*' she murmured in the throatiest, sexiest murmur she could muster. Then looked up into his eyes and pouted, as if inviting a kiss in return.

CHAPTER FIVE

TAKEN UNAWARES, LUKAS froze at Ashleigh's touch. For a heart-stopping moment she stayed intimately close, her curves against his chest, her sweetly scented hair tickling his face. She whispered in his ear, her voice laced with amusement at his reaction. 'Try to look like you're enjoying this—we're meant to be in love.'

Then she sat down on her chair opposite him, flashing a radiant smile to the waiter as she thanked him for his elaborate play at shaking out her linen napkin and placing it on her lap.

'Bella inglese,' the waiter murmured in Italian—*beautiful English lady.*

Lukas thought that was far too fulsome a compliment to *his* date. Besides, Ashleigh was Australian not English. Though he could not blame the waiter for his mistake; with her copper hair, pale skin and blue eyes, Ashleigh looked like she belonged in this country.

She had flung herself into playing her part as his girlfriend with gusto. Now *he* had to take up the role of doting boyfriend.

Ashleigh was right. Tonight was a rehearsal for tomorrow. He should react like a man smitten with a woman. Trouble was, that would be only too easy. He had allowed himself to get entranced by her closeness. By her fresh, warm scent. The touch of her lovely mouth on his cheek. By the sudden, sensual awareness her closeness had aroused.

He'd been too shocked by his body's reaction to respond in his fake date role. The waiter wasn't wrong—*she was beautiful*. And way more enticing than he had expected. He would have to rein in his libido if he were to remain as impartial as he needed to be to play this game. *It was all pretend.*

'Of course,' he said. He reached over across the table to take both her hands in his, look deep into her eyes. 'It's good to be here with you, *agápi mou*. I've had a long, stressful day.'

'My day has been quite exciting,' she murmured. 'Especially when you found me without any clothes on and…' He knew she was referring to the incident in his bathtub but, the way she murmured it, any person overhearing her would assume she was referring to something rather more intimate. If only they'd heard how she'd screeched at him.

'Now we can relax over a good meal,' he said. He released her hands, realising he had held them for a moment longer than was required for play-acting.

Ashleigh's lips curved up into a smile that hinted at her dimples. 'That's more like it,' she whispered. 'The more practice we get in this evening, the less we risk seeming stilted tomorrow. What if someone you know saw us behaving like it's a business meeting? Which I guess it is, in a way.' *Did she feel even the slightest stirring of what he was feeling?*

'Business? Yes, it is and the interplay between us must be believable,' he said. But he would have to remain on guard against the attraction he felt towards her. He did not want any distractions from the main game, which was—as always—the business. 'We have to get this charade right—it's important I seal that deal with Tina Norris.'

'Tina Norris? That's the…the cougar's name?'

He kept his voice low as he spoke. His business dealings were not for public broadcast. 'She's the CEO of a major distributor of domestic appliances and consumer electronic products to retailers, businesses, hotels, property developers and so on. Tina inherited the business from her father, then nearly lost it in a nasty divorce.'

Ashleigh's face softened with sympathy. 'The poor woman—how awful for her.'

Lucas put up a warning hand. 'Don't go feeling sorry for her. Tina Norris is a barracuda. But she is formidably effective in her business and I see a synergy between our two companies. I want to get on board with the Norris group.'

He thought of Ashleigh's perceptive comment. *On board* with Tina but not *in bed* with her. He could not share with Ashleigh—or anyone— the scars of an old aversion that made even the thought of sexual advances from cougar Tina send shudders up his spine.

He'd been fourteen, already tall and well-built with a man's body but still with the heart and soul and idealism of a boy. At one of his parents' infamous parties, his mother's friend had stumbled into his bedroom, drunk. He'd been too naïve to recognise she'd had seduction on her mind. When she'd made her intentions clear he'd been repulsed—and frightened. His shouts had brought his parents to his room. His mother—drunk herself—had found it amusing. His father had mocked him—he'd thought his son was a fool to pass up an opportunity for initiation by a skilled older woman. They had not protected him.

'That's what tomorrow night will be all about—securing a business connection, while playing down any personal relationship with Tina,' he concluded.

Ashleigh nodded. 'That's good to know so I have an idea of what she's like. Now I have to find out as much as I can about you. And you me, of course.'

He leaned over. 'There's one important thing you should know about me.'

Ashleigh quirked a perfectly arched auburn eyebrow. 'And that is?'

'I get irritable when I'm hungry.'

She smiled. 'Is that a hint that you'd like to order? Because I can't stop looking at that impressive antipasto display.'

By the time he and Ashleigh had returned to

their table, their plates laden with a selection of Italian salami, prosciutto, marinated octopus, roasted vegetables, cheeses and olives, he was feeling more relaxed. The waiter took their orders for the next course and they settled back to eat.

Lukas noticed Ashleigh was hungry. Although she ate her starter slowly, he could see she was holding back, pretending restraint. If he wasn't there, he suspected the plate would be emptied very quickly and she'd be back up at the antipasto table for a second helping. He wondered when she'd last eaten.

'Why are you so short of money?' he asked her. 'You're educated, you held a responsible job.'

Startled, she stopped with a spear of asparagus that had been wrapped in prosciutto halfway to her mouth. She put it back onto her plate with a look of regret. 'Because I cancelled my wedding so close to the date of the ceremony. There were consequences. Hefty deposits on the venue and the catering that were not refundable. An unworn wedding gown to pay for. It was a considerable burden to bear on my own.'

He frowned. 'Surely your fiancé was also responsible for the debt?'

She shook her head. 'It was my fault there was no wedding. He didn't see that he should pay for my "rash" decision.'

'He was unhappy you called it off?'

'Very unhappy.' She looked down at her plate.

Lukas could understand that. Even on this short acquaintance he could see how a man could be captivated by Ashleigh Murphy. Not him, of course. He was beyond being mesmerised by a beautiful woman. Especially a woman like this. In his assessment, he realised she was not the type for a no-strings fling—which was the only kind of relationship he did these days. Yet there was something appealing about her. There were attractive women everywhere in this restaurant. But none that caught his attention. His eyes were only drawn to Ashleigh, the backpacker he'd found in his bathtub.

'Did your fiancé not try to get you to reconsider?' he asked.

'My *ex*-fiancé, you mean. He begged me to change my mind,' she said, with a twist to her mouth that spoke not of regret but of something else. Irritation? Contempt, even? 'But I wouldn't. No one would believe me that I didn't want to marry him. Not him. Not my family. Not even the marriage celebrant—whose fee I also had to pay, by the way.'

'That seems unfair.'

'I think so too. If Dan were the gentleman he claims to be, he would have paid his share. But it's the house that has really crippled me.'

'The house?'

'It seemed a good idea to buy a house together for us to live in after the wedding. I put up my share of the deposit, signed the mortgage documents. My savings are all tied up in the house.'

'Why don't you sell the house if there is to be no marriage?'

'Dan refuses to put it on the market. Why, I don't know. I will *never* live in that house.'

Lukas had some sympathy for her faraway fiancé. To be so close to securing this lovely woman as his wife, only to have her run away. No wonder the man was unhappy. However, he doubted the break was as final as Ashleigh said it was. He had learned from bitter experience that a woman could claim to be free while still being very much entangled with another man. Lukas would not be surprised if this Dan turned up in

London to take her back. 'Perhaps he's hoping you will return.'

'He'll be hoping for ever, if that's the case. Ironically, it was buying the house that was the beginning of the end for me. I wanted to live at the beach. Can you believe when a house next door to my parents went on sale he wanted us to buy that? I had to fight for the beach house. Why I didn't back out then I don't know.'

She shook her head in disbelief and a strand of her bright hair worked its way free from its constraint and fell across her cheek. Lukas fought the urge to reach over and push it back off her face. If Ashleigh were a real date he wouldn't hesitate to touch her in such an intimate manner—but this was all pretend. He kept his hands firmly on his side of the table.

'In traditional Greek culture it would be seen as admirable for a woman to live close to her parents,' he said. He chose to live in central Athens, in the shadow of the Acropolis, away from his parents in the leafy green suburb where the wealthiest families congregated.

Ashleigh scowled—an expression that, far from being forbidding, looked cute on her. 'It doesn't work like that where I come from. I want to be independent of my parents, not living in their pockets. And wouldn't you think a husband would want his new wife to himself?'

Oh, yes. If he had a woman like this for his wife he would not share her with anyone. Not that he *ever* wanted a wife. The example of his parents and others in their social set had turned him right off marriage. The sickening hypocrisy of it all. That last summer of freedom on the islands, there had been a girl—a beautiful, vivacious French girl named Céline who had inspired in him thoughts of love and commitment and family. But the painful way it had ended had extinguished any such thoughts from his heart. Nothing and no one had since breathed life into those ashes.

'Most men would want privacy with their bride,' he said, in what he hoped was a non-committal manner.

Her scowl deepened. 'It was when he tried to bulldoze me into buying that house that I realised how stultifying it would be to be married to Dan,' she continued. 'He eventually agreed to the beach house but I knew even as I signed the documents that I shouldn't be. I'd be stepping straight into middle age. My dreams would be totally subsumed by his limited vision. I *had* to get away.'

'So you came to London?'

'And here I'm staying. Though of course my family don't believe me. They think I'll go crawling back to Dan.'

He frowned. 'Why would they think that?'

She looked down at her plate. 'Because I'd broken up with him before and gone back.' She looked back up at Lukas, her mouth twisted. 'More than once, actually. Mistake compounded by mistake, I see now.'

He paused. 'Then perhaps you will return to him.'

'Never,' she said with such vehemence her eyes seemed to spark blue fire.

He didn't believe her. A woman could lie so convincingly that the boyfriend or fiancé or ex-husband meant nothing. Never again would he let himself get caught up—even for the most casual of liaisons—with a woman who was still involved with another man. Not that Ashleigh's ties to her so-called former fiancé back in Australia affected him at all. He wouldn't see her again after tomorrow night.

Just then their main courses arrived—steamed sea bass for him and organic chicken with balsamic vinegar reduction for her. The meal was complemented with a dry white wine from Tuscany. Ashleigh's eyes lit up at the sight of her plate. He doubted she would still be hungry after that.

When she pushed back her plate with a sigh of satisfaction and some food still left on it, he was pleased. She needed someone to care for her.

Ashleigh reached over and put her hand on his forearm in a gesture that to other eyes would seem affectionate and familiar. 'Thank you,' she said. 'I can't remember when I had such an excellent meal.'

Any meal more like it, from the way she'd polished off that chicken. He couldn't help but worry about her. How could she survive in one of the most expensive cities in the world on a maid's income?

'Would you like dessert?'

'Not for me,' she said.

'Or me,' he said. He was disciplined with his

eating and exercise. And kept an iron-clad guard on his emotions. His heart had been battered once too often by the betrayal of the parents who should have protected him, by the careless cruelty of Céline.

Ashleigh treated him to her enchanting smile. 'I noticed you sneaking a glance at your watch. I know you've had a big day. But there are a few more things I wanted to ask you about yourself.'

'Fire away,' he said.

'Do you have brothers or sisters?'

'I'm an only child.' So often as a lonely, confused child he'd longed for a companion. Though it was as well his parents had not been entrusted with the care of a daughter. As an adult, he'd wished he'd had someone on his side to help sort out the mess of the once thriving business his parents had inherited from his grandfather. 'You?'

'An older sister. She's six years older than me. When I was born she thought I was her baby. She still thinks I'm her baby.' The edge of irritation to her voice hinted at ongoing conflict with her family. She was older than he had at first thought. But she seemed to have the desperate need for independence of someone younger. It intrigued him, but he did not want to be intrigued by her. She was here to serve a purpose and that was all.

'How long have you been in London?' he asked.

'Three weeks,' she said.

'Good. That's long enough,' he said.

Her brow pleated to a frown. 'For what?'

'For us to have met and started to date—theoretically, that is,' he said. 'To try and pretend we've known each other for longer could be disastrous.'

She nodded. 'Good point. As far as Tina Norris is concerned, we met shortly after I arrived in London. Were you actually in London then?'

'No. But I could have been. She wouldn't know otherwise.'

'That's the timing sorted. What about the place we met—theoretically, of course?'

She screwed up her face in a delightful expression of concentration. 'I'm thinking about where I went as soon as I got here. All the tourist places, of course. The museums and art galleries. Big Ben. The Tower of London—I adored the Tower. Oxford Street. Not likely to be places where you would be.' She paused. 'I did a lot of walking around, just taking in the atmosphere, the Christmas lights, the shop windows. It's feasible we could have bumped into each other.' She smiled. 'I've had a light-bulb moment. Didn't you say you were at The Shard today?'

'My meeting this afternoon with Tina was there, yes.'

'How about we met in the bar at The Shard? One time I went there with Sophie. There were guys like you in suits, guys who—'

'Wanted to buy you a drink?' *Of course they did.*

'Exactly. Why couldn't one of those guys have been you?'

'Did you accept a drink from one of them?' This could *not* be an inexplicable surge of jealousy.

'No. I'd just run away from my wedding and was in no mood to meet men. Getting picked up by a guy in a bar—even such a salubrious bar—was the last thing I wanted.'

'And now?'

'I want to be single. Being half of a couple for so long was like being caught in a trap that was slowly strangling me. I'm happy to *pretend* to be your date. In real life, I'm not interested in dating anyone. I just want to be *me*.'

More and more, Ashleigh sounded like the ideal pretend date. He couldn't have found anyone more suitable if he'd gone looking. She would not make any demands on him. Not want to turn fake into real. There'd be no dramas and wounded feelings when he ended things with her. He would take her to dinner tomorrow night, let her stay the night at his house and then *goodbye, Ashleigh*.

'Meeting at The Shard is an excellent idea for a cover story,' he said.

'That's settled, then,' she said. 'Next step is to get things straight about how it all went down.'

He thought for a moment. 'I was visiting London and met a business associate for a drink. He went home. I noticed you with your friend.'

'You asked me would I like a drink.' Whether unconsciously or not, Ashleigh had adopted a flirtatious manner, eyes widened, head thrown back, lips pouting. *Enticing.* That was the word for her.

'And you immediately said yes.'

'How could I refuse?' she said. 'I was so impressed by your Greek handsomeness and charming manner.' The flirtatiousness came naturally to her. He could see how a man could become ensnared. Lucky this charade was only for two nights.

He smiled. 'Is handsomeness actually a word in English?'

'If it isn't it should be. You are very handsome. In real life if you'd asked to buy me a drink I might even have said yes.'

'I'm flattered.' Oddly enough, he was. He tried to think of a compliment he could return to her without seeming overly effusive. Whatever he came up with sounded either mundane or too much.

She tilted her head to one side. 'I'm waiting.'

He frowned. 'For what?'

'I'm giving you a prompt: now you're meant to say you were smitten by my beauty.'

He hadn't thought of that. 'I was smitten by your beauty,' he repeated in a monotone, fighting the smile twitching at the corners of his mouth.

'Not like that! With meaning,' she said, a little crossly. Then stopped. 'You have to take this seriously, you know. It won't work if you don't.

After all, it was your idea and it's your business deal at stake.'

He was grateful for the reminder. *This was just a business deal.* He leaned across the table to her. So close their heads nearly touched. He looked deep into her incredibly blue eyes, purposefully made his voice a tone deeper and seductive. 'I was smitten by your beauty, your gorgeous hair, your perfect skin, your shapely body. Then intrigued by your Australianness.'

'I…er…don't think that's an actual word,' she said and her voice wasn't quite steady.

'It's a word now,' he said.

Then he reached out and smoothed the errant lock of bright hair from her face, his fingers lingering on her smooth skin as he tucked it behind her ear. She flushed and shivered at his touch. Her eyes glittered all shades of blue. He couldn't help but remember how she'd looked in his bathtub, naked but for those bubbles. At the powerful rush of awareness, he withdrew his hand as if he'd come much too close to a flame.

'Th…that's more like it,' she said. 'I think we can…can make it look like we are actually attracted to each other without too much trouble.'

'Indeed we can,' he said. It would be *hiding* his attraction that would be the problem. He leaned back in his chair, still shaken by his reaction. 'One more thing,' he said. 'What were you wearing when I met you in the bar at The Shard?'

She indicated her black dress. 'This dress.'

'Not jeans?'

'No.'

'Or trainers?'

'Of course not.'

'And your anorak?' He couldn't keep the distaste from his voice.

'It was in the cloakroom.' She frowned. 'Where is this leading to?'

He shook his head. 'Your clothes. They won't do. A woman like Tina Norris would never be convinced you're my girlfriend if you dress like a maid.'

'This is actually my waitress dress but I get what you mean,' she said, with a downward droop of her mouth.

'It's a nice enough dress, but you should be wearing designer fashion.'

'I can't afford—'

He didn't like the crestfallen look on her face

that his words had caused. 'I know you can't. Which is why I will take you shopping tomorrow to ensure you're suitably dressed. At my expense.'

Her eyes widened. 'Take me shopping? Buy me clothes? But you can't do that. I... I can't accept clothes from you. It wouldn't be right.'

A woman who didn't jump at the chance of a wealthy man wielding a credit card? Ashleigh really was very different from the women he usually associated with. Women who revelled in the lifestyle his wealth could give them. Who were placated by a gift of expensive jewellery when he ended things with them.

'I can and you will,' he said. 'I want this deal to go through. You have to be dressed appropriately. End of story.'

'I... I don't know what to say,' she said, raising troubled eyes to his.

'"Yes" will do,' he said. 'I will take you shopping in Bond Street tomorrow morning.'

Then he leaned over to kiss her lightly on the cheek. 'Relax and enjoy it, *agápi mou*.'

CHAPTER SIX

ASHLEIGH WAS NOT the kind of person to be easily intimidated. But she'd learned on her first few days in London that a look from the snooty shop assistants on London's super-posh Bond Street could shrivel her ego to the size of a thimble.

Her friend Sophie lived and breathed fashion. Ashleigh was as interested in clothes and shoes as most women, but her knowledge of luxury, high-end labels extended to what she saw in glossy magazines at the hairdresser.

Sophie had taken Ashleigh window-shopping not long after she'd arrived. Together they'd traipsed the length of combined Old Bond Street and New Bond Street—Ashleigh looking around her in awe. She'd rubbernecked at the opulent elegance of the Victorian era Royal Arcade. Stopped to stare at the Christmas decorations. Sophie told her that Bond Street was one of the most expensive shopping streets in the world and she could well believe it. It was lined with elegant shops, each more luxurious than the last. Each show-cased luxury labels—some of which Ashleigh had heard of, others she'd had no idea existed. Not just clothes but accessories, shoes, jewellery, even chocolates.

'I can't afford to buy anything in these designer shops,' Sophie had explained. 'But I like to look. Not to copy ideas for my own designs but to note details like the cut of a collar or the placement of a pocket and to swoon over the beautiful fabrics.'

'One day it will be your designs people will be swooning over,' Ashleigh had said loyally. She had always believed in her friend's talent—right back to when they were schoolgirls in Manchester and Sophie had been so welcoming to the new girl from Australia.

On that shopping day with Sophie, Ashleigh had dared to venture into one shop to ask the price of a belt she thought her sister would like. She'd nearly fainted at the price the saleswoman had quoted—and the look of disdain delivered at her along with it.

'Big mistake,' Sophie had hissed on their way out. 'These people think if you have to ask the price you can't afford to shop there. The way to behave is to look at everything with equal disdain—be as snooty as they are right back at them.'

Ashleigh had laughed. 'I don't know that I can do disdain. Especially when everything in these shops is so wonderful. I can only dream that I could ever buy anything here.'

Now she was discovering that shopping on Bond Street in the company of billionaire Lukas Christophedes was an altogether different experience.

It started with the discreetly luxurious limousine and chauffeur that picked her and Lukas up from the townhouse to drive them into the heart of London. 'The driver will keep the car somewhere nearby, ready to load with your parcels,' Lukas explained.

'Parcels? Aren't we buying just a dress for me to wear tonight?' Ashleigh asked.

'You're out with me in public as my girlfriend. You have to look the part. Our first stop will be for clothes for you to change into immediately.'

'You mean shop for clothes to go shopping in?'

'Yes.'

Was he serious? A thrill of excitement ran through her. She'd seen so many clothes she'd coveted that day with Sophie. Now she might get to try them on.

She was sitting next to Lukas in the back seat of the car, the seat so wide there was no danger of any accidental touching. Not that she was worried that Lukas would cross boundaries. She'd locked her bedroom door last night, just in case she had misread the situation with him, but she need not have worried. It was she who had lain awake for some time, imagining him lying alone in the enormous bed in his room down the corridor, his long limbs and powerful body sprawled across the sheets. *Did he sleep naked?*

At the *ristorante* when he'd leaned across to tuck her hair back from her face, she'd felt a jolt of attraction so powerful that it had rendered her momentarily speechless. When she'd agreed to his deal—not that she'd had much choice—she hadn't expected *that.* It was disconcerting, to say the least.

But he had shown every sign of being a gentleman. It was her who'd been bothered by fantasies of him naked in bed just a few rooms away. But when she'd eventually drifted off to sleep it was with a warm sense of security and she'd slept better than she had on her first illicit two nights alone in his house.

'Is that really necessary? I'll be wearing your mother's gorgeous coat when I get out of this nice warm car.'

'But when you take it off your black work trousers give you away.'

'They're not bad trousers,' she protested. 'And the shirt is new.'

'Straight from the high street,' he said.

'Yes,' she said, her voice trailing away. Up until this moment she'd thought shopping in the big high street chains was as exciting as her shopping would ever get. Now, the way Lukas said it, 'high street' sounded like an insult. Did she really look that bad? The answer would have to be yes if she was to be mingling with billionaires.

He seemed to sense her sudden stab of insecurity. 'If you're performing in a play, you have to be in the right costume, yes? Think of this as getting your wardrobe right and enjoy it.'

Lukas as wardrobe master? Why not?

'Let the fun begin,' she said, determined to put

aside any qualms she had about a man who was still very much a stranger buying her clothes. After all, she would move out of the maid's bedroom tomorrow and leave her borrowed finery behind her. Then she would never see him again.

For the first time she felt a pang of regret about that. He was an extraordinarily attractive man. She wished… *No.* There was no point in wishing they had met under different circumstances. That would never have happened—not the maid and the billionaire.

Excitement began to buzz through her as the car turned into Bond Street. When she'd visited with Sophie, they'd come by Tube. Did coming with Lukas in a chauffeur-driven car make the Christmas decorations shine brighter? She stared in wonder at the sight of a famous jewellery store completely wrapped in glittering Christmas ribbon like a multi-million-dollar festive parcel. Other shops glittered and shone with decorations in among the flags that flew above to proclaim the famous labels. She craned her head to see if the theatrical works of art in the shop display windows had changed since her last visit. Regent Street with its famous Christmas decorations was only a street away. She must come back soon in the evening to see this area at its festive best.

The closer it got to Christmas, the more people there were on the street. Everywhere she looked, fashionably dressed people—men as well as women—swept past on the narrow pavements, their arms strung with shopping bags emblazoned with famous designer labels. Whatever dress she ended up with, Ashleigh vowed, she would keep the bag as a souvenir.

The limousine dropped them off outside the starkly minimalist store of a well-known European designer label. It glided off, no doubt to join the other limousines double parked along the street. Ashleigh wrapped the beautiful leopard print coat around her like armour. Last time she'd been here she'd been wearing the past-its-use-by-date anorak.

'We should be able to quickly find something for you to change into in here,' Lukas said as he swept her into the shop with arrogant assurance. She thrilled at the feeling that nothing and no one intimidated this man. Certainly not a shop assistant. That particular brand of wimpishness belonged to Ashleigh.

Lukas exuded an air of wealth and confidence. A well groomed young female shop assistant almost tripped over her stilettos in an effort to reach him before her colleagues did. She'd probably assessed the cost of his suit and the value of his watch as he'd walked through the door.

Ashleigh stood meekly by his side—not that she usually did meek but she was too overwhelmed to be anything but subdued. She shifted from foot to foot, not sure of how this would work. She glanced up at Lukas. Would he choose what she wore or would she have a say in her play-acting wardrobe?

The assistant welcomed Lukas almost to the point of fawning on him. But Ashleigh didn't miss the sideways narrowed glance directed at her. The woman actually folded her arms in front of her and looked her up and down—out of the line of Lukas's sight, of course. As she did, Ashleigh recognised her as one of the people who had been dismissive of her and Sophie when they'd ventured into this shop on their window-shopping day. That crossed arm thing had annoyed her then and it annoyed her now.

'My friend has just arrived from Australia and

needs some winter clothes,' Lukas said. It went without saying that he would be picking up the tab.

Again that sideward glance. Ashleigh realised the woman couldn't place her. She had immediately sized up her bargain basement shoes and clothes, noted the anomaly of the designer coat and speculated about her relationship to Lukas.

She thinks I'm his mistress, Ashleigh realised. Or worse—that he was buying her in some way. She got the distinct impression she was being judged as inferior to the handsome tall man beside her.

While Ashleigh might have been intimidated into *meek* she was never going to do *inferior.* And right now, as Sophie had suggested, she determined to muster up an attitude of disdain.

She straightened her shoulders and lifted her chin. Schooling her face into a mask of critical indifference, she let her gaze wander across the featureless mannequins dressed in various minimalist garments in tones of grey and winter white. She took a step towards the chrome racks with their artful displays of just a few garments, not deigning to pull anything close for an inspection.

Then she looked back up at Lukas. 'Nothing appeals, I'm afraid, darling,' she said finally. The clothes were fabulous but Bond Street was full of shops like this and surely her presence by Lukas's side demanded a better attitude.

His dark brows rose. 'Are you sure? We've only just got here and I wanted you to have a complete new wardrobe more suitable for this cold weather.'

She dimpled up at him. 'Quite sure.' She met the barely disguised dismay of the assistant. She hoped the woman regretted her bad manners as much as she was no doubt regretting her lost commission.

'Whatever you want, *agápi mou*,' he said, turning on his heel.

'I think I'll find what I want a few doors up,' Ashleigh said, naming an equally well-known designer. Then she tucked her arm through Lukas's and stalked out of the store.

Back out on the pavement, she smiled at him. 'Sorry about that, but I didn't want to give any business to someone who was so judgemental and downright rude. Did you see the way she looked at me?' She kept her arm tucked in his, liking the feeling, unable to stop herself from wondering what it would be like to have the real-life right to walk arm in arm with him.

'My mother always swears you get better service if you already look the part,' he said. 'I guess she's right.' Ashleigh appreciated that there was no hint of *I told you so* in his voice.

'Your mother sounds interesting,' Ashleigh said. 'Her taste in coats is excellent, that's for sure.'

'She's certainly an expert shopper,' he said drily.

The reception was so much better at their next stop. A courteous sales associate introduced herself first to Ashleigh and then to Lukas and listened as Ashleigh explained her needs.

The woman handed Lukas over to another associate, who settled him in a comfortable chair and asked him if he would like a coffee. Ashleigh found herself ushered into a roomy, beautifully furnished changing room. Her sales associate returned with a choice of garments for her to try. She felt giddy at the number of zeros on the price tags but reminded herself that, as far as Lukas was concerned, anything he purchased was an investment in a potentially lucrative business deal. *Enjoy every minute of this,* she told herself, *it will never happen again.*

Finally, she settled on a pair of perfectly cut slim black trousers with a narrow belt, and a fine knit cashmere and silk sweater in a flattering shade of charcoal. They were perfect under the leopard print coat. She didn't dare look at the price tags—though she had a very good idea of what just the belt alone would cost.

The sales associate asked if she would like to show Lukas what she had chosen. It was her only discreet reference that she realised who would be paying the bill.

Ashleigh tiptoed out of the changing room. Lukas was engrossed in the thoughtfully provided newspaper. What if this were for real and this handsome man waiting for her really was hers? That he would notice she was there and give her that slow smile she already found so compelling? The thought gave her an unwarranted shiver of excitement. But she could not let herself forget for even an instant that this was all a charade.

'What do you think?' she asked.

He looked up, startled. She couldn't read all the expressions that flashed across his face but admiration was certainly one of them. She flushed at the intensity of his gaze. 'Good,' he said. 'But you need boots. Black high-heeled boots.'

Ashleigh and her helpful sales associate were only too happy to oblige.

Lukas was both pleased and amused at the way Ashleigh sashayed into the designer shops with so much more confidence. She looked sensational. The tight trousers showed off her shapely behind and slender legs, the boots gave a sexy sway to her walk—and he wasn't immune to the effect.

He wasn't the only one to notice. Heads turned to watch the beautiful, stylishly dressed redhead. Lukas realised that it wasn't just her that commanded attention—together they must make a striking couple. The realisation made him feel proud. He congratulated himself for seeing the potential in the scruffy backpacker.

But, with an unlimited credit card at her disposal, he couldn't understand why she needed to go into so *many* shops in search of an appropriate dress for the dinner tonight.

He wanted Ashleigh to get it right—both for his sake and her own as she could wear the dress on future occasions. Those occasions could well be far away in Australia when she got over her snit about her wedding and went back to her fiancé. Lucky guy, he thought, a touch morosely.

But shopping was far from Lukas's favourite pastime. He was going to have to call a halt to it. 'Surely it can't be that difficult to find a suitable outfit for tonight,' he grumbled. 'I can't endure any more hanging around while you look at every damn dress the shops stock.'

Her eyes widened. 'You did tell me to relax and enjoy it,' she said. 'And enjoy it I am. But if you're getting bored there is a dress I could go back to. It's not perfect but I like it and—'

'I'm not bored,' he said.

Actually, he *was* bored by the interminable waiting around. When he shopped, his mission was to spend as little time as possible with the shop assistant or the tailor and he made instant decisions. But he wasn't bored with Ashleigh.

Not in the slightest. In fact her enthusiasm and pleasure in the experience was refreshing and somehow endearing. Then there was her total lack of greed.

'One more shop, okay?' she said beguilingly.

'I've created a shopping monster,' he grumbled again, though he didn't really mean it. Shopping with Ashleigh was the closest thing to fun he could remember having with a woman.

He followed her to the next shop and realised it was the one where his mother must have bought the coat Ashleigh was wearing. She realised it at the same time, her face lighting up. 'This is a good omen,' she said.

It seemed it was.

Once inside the store, his fake girlfriend looked around her and sighed a happy sigh. 'I love everything in here,' she said. 'I think I'm in fashion heaven.'

Even the poker-faced sales associate cracked a smile at that and was soon leading Ashleigh away to the fitting room.

Just minutes later Ashleigh emerged. 'I think I've found the ideal dress,' she said, giving her model-like twirl. 'It comes in black but I prefer the plum. What do you think?' She paused, waiting for his reaction.

Lukas caught his breath at how lovely she looked. The short, deep purple dress was deceptively simple. But it clung subtly to her curves and hugged her waist and her pale skin was luminous in contrast. He must have stared too long without comment.

'Do you like it?' she asked, a note of uncertainty creeping into her voice.

'Yes,' he said.

She pointed her foot in front of her like a dancer. 'And the shoes? Do you approve?'

The dress was discreetly sensual but the shoes were sexy as hell—a staggeringly high-heeled stiletto in narrow, multi-coloured leather stripes that buckled around her ankles.

He had to clear his throat to answer. 'Yes,' he said again, unable to choke out anything more.

'I'll take that as approval,' she said with a curve of a smile to him and a nod to the sales associate. 'Please tell me you're not just saying that because you're sick of shopping?'

'No. Just buy the dress. And the shoes.'

Then the sales assistant—no doubt scenting a

generous credit card—came bearing a selection
of glittering jewellery—semi-precious stones but
still expensive.

'May I suggest these?' The woman fastened
a necklace of large purple stones set in silver
around Ashleigh's throat, a smaller version
around her wrist. The jewellery lifted the simple dress and was perfect with her blue eyes and
red hair.

'She'll take them,' he said.

'Thank you,' she breathed. 'Thank you, *darling*,' she remembered to add.

Ashleigh's new look was classy and discreetly
sensual—a most appropriate look for his consort. Tina Norris couldn't possibly imagine he
could be interested in another woman when she
saw him with Ashleigh. He couldn't endure the
thought of having to repel unwanted advances
from the older woman. It brought back all those
unpleasant, frightening memories.

'Is that it?' he asked Ashleigh.

'I…uh… I still need to buy the right underwear
for this dress. I can get it here.' She flushed high
on her cheekbones and couldn't meet his gaze.

What kind of underwear? A sheer, lacy bra

cupping her breasts, the triangle of skimpy panties defining her hips? Or might she emerge from the fitting room in nothing but a tightly laced black corset, a tiny thong and those high-heeled black boots—then do a slow twirl and ask him, all wide-eyed: *What do you think?*

Lukas clenched his fists by his sides. *Damn it.* If he hadn't first seen her wearing nothing but bubbles, thoughts like this might not plague him.

Perspiration broke out on his forehead and he had to drag a finger around a collar that felt suddenly tight. The shop was overheated. He had to get out of here. She needed a watch to replace the chunky digital thing more suitable for a tracksuit than an elegant dress. Time could be saved if he chose one for her.

'You get what you need—' he couldn't actually utter the word *underwear* '—while I shoot out to another shop.'

The associate held up an unstructured wool coat in a delicate shade of lavender that would complement the dress perfectly. '*Yes* to that too,' he said. 'And leather gloves.'

Ashleigh leaned forward, giving him a glimpse of the swell of her pale breasts in the clinging dress. *She wasn't wearing a bra.* Her fresh sweet perfume wafted up to him, heady and exciting. 'Are you sure about the coat? It's expensive and not really necessary for one night and—'

'Just get it,' he said through gritted teeth before he strode towards the door.

By the time he got back with the watch in the pocket of his coat, Ashleigh was covered up again in her new black trousers and top. But once he'd imagined what she might look like in her underwear it was difficult to get the sensual images out of his head.

He paid for Ashleigh's purchases and picked up the collection of heavy paper bags emblazoned with the designer label. 'I'll carry these out to the car.'

She put her hand on his arm to stop him. 'Please, let me,' she begged. 'I'll probably never shop here again in my life and I want to enjoy every bit of the experience.'

Ashleigh walked back out of the shop in triumph, bearing her haul of bags like trophies for all the other well-heeled shoppers to take note. She seemed exhilarated, cheeks flushed, eyes glinting in triumph and Lukas realised she was on a shopping high, fired by a pleasure that was almost orgasmic.

He had to force away thoughts of what she might look like flushed with ecstasy in his arms. He gritted his teeth. This awareness of her as a woman rather than a pawn in his business strategy with Tina Norris could not go on.

Lukas signalled to his driver and the car pulled up in front of them. With her hovering around him, he placed Ashleigh's parcels in the boot, obeying her admonishments to be careful with the precious cargo.

Then he turned to her. 'This is where I leave you,' he said, more abruptly than he'd intended. He didn't know whether to be pleased or perturbed at the disappointment that drooped her expression.

'Where are you—?'

'I have business to attend to in the city,' he said.

'Oh. I can catch the bus back to Chelsea,' she said. 'That is, if it's okay for me to be there while you're not there. I—'

Lukas put up his hand to halt her flow of words. He'd known enough high maintenance women to realise that getting the clothes right wasn't the end of it.

'The driver is at your disposal. First to take you to a hairdresser and beauty salon in Mayfair, just near here, where I've made you an appointment. Then back to Chelsea.'

He was treated to the full dazzle of her dimples. 'Seriously? I was worried about my hair; it really needs styling and I—'

'Get done whatever you need to get done,' he said with a dismissive wave. 'The driver knows where to take you. Just be home in plenty of time for our dinner date with Tina Norris.'

'Of course I will. I mean, that's what it's all about. Your business deal.'

He turned to walk away but was stopped by her hand on his elbow.

She looked up at him, her cheeks still flushed pink with excitement. 'Lukas? I know this will all be over in the morning. But thank you. This has been one of the most wonderful experiences of my life. Like a fairy tale. I'll never forget my day shopping on Bond Street with my fairy godfather.' She paused. 'Well, not *fairy* godfather. I didn't mean you... Heck, you know what I mean.'

Then she flung her arms around him and kissed him on the cheek. 'Just thank you.'

He was too bemused to do anything but watch while she slid gracefully into the car as if accustomed to being driven in luxury around London. Shoppers brushed past him but for a long time he just stood there, remembering the warmth of her arms, the touch of her lips, and feeling dazed and inexplicably bereft. Then he turned on his heel and strode into the crowd.

CHAPTER SEVEN

POWERFUL, POISED AND PREDATORY—that was Ashleigh's first impression of Tina Norris.

The glamorous forty-something woman narrowed her eyes when Lukas introduced her as his girlfriend. There was speculation and suspicion there, but also a flash of disappointment. Ashleigh smiled a greeting but immediately felt on guard. She took a deep breath to steady her nerves. An award-winning performance would be required of her tonight. Thank heaven she was dressed for the part, with her new designer clothes and the confidence of newly styled hair and professional make-up.

As a child, Ashleigh had known of Mayfair in central London as the most valuable stop on the board in the game of Monopoly. Since then, she'd heard the area described as a haven for the international super-rich. That certainly fitted the description of Lukas. And while Tina was as British as could be, she too was very wealthy. Lukas had chosen the restaurant for tonight's dinner because Tina had an apartment nearby, although her home and company headquarters were in Liverpool.

And then there was Ashleigh Murphy—recently of downtown Bundaberg, more recently of no fixed abode, tomorrow to have no abode at all.

As the waiter led them from the bar area where they'd met Tina to seat them at their table, Ashleigh managed to catch Lukas's eye. The message was clear—they'd better get their story right.

The critically acclaimed restaurant was elegant, the Christmas decorations subdued in shades of silver. Their table was set with crisp linen and gleaming crystal, the floor carpeted so it was quiet enough for a non-shouted conversation. Unobtrusive waiters glided silently between tables.

'Nice,' said Tina, looking around her with critical brown eyes. 'Although I'm not too sure what to expect from the Scandinavian-Japanese fusion menu.'

'It's not a cuisine I've tried,' said Ashleigh.

'I don't think too many people have,' said Tina.

Did that imply criticism of Lukas for his choice of restaurant? Ashleigh decided to let the comment go. It was her role to support her pretend boyfriend, not to be combative on his behalf. She would just watch, listen and play her part when required. And not order the fried fish skin.

It didn't take long for Ashleigh to decide Tina was a little too much—too blonde, too tanned, too much cosmetic intervention and too blunt for comfort. Did that bluntness come from an overdose of self-assurance or because Tina knew it would put her on edge? The older woman started her inquisition as soon as they were all three seated at the circular table. 'So why have you kept Ashleigh a secret, Lukas?' she asked.

Lukas looked stunned at such a directly personal question so early in the evening. Ashleigh jumped in to rescue him. She placed her recently manicured hand over his where it rested on the table.

'Hardly a secret,' she murmured. 'It's just so new we've wanted to spend all our time… well…alone together.' His hand was warm and strong under hers—she liked the feeling. Liked it too much.

Tina's perfectly pencilled brows rose. 'How new?' she asked then back-pedalled as if she realised her question could be construed as intrusive. 'I mean, when I do business with people I like to get to know their partners. I wasn't aware you had a lady in your life, Lukas.'

'I didn't until recently,' he said.

Ashleigh had decided that the closer to the truth their story, the better it would stick. 'We've only known each other for three weeks,' she said. 'I was meant to be in London for a two-week vacation. Then I met Lukas quite by chance.' She curled her hand over his and edged as close as she could to him. Would it be too much to drop a kiss on his cheek? Perhaps it would be overkill at this early stage. 'I decided to stay in the UK.'

'As you would,' said Tina with a cynical twist to her mouth that made Ashleigh cringe. The implication was clear. *Gold-digger.* 'Where did you two meet?' The question was quick and direct, as if intended to put Ashleigh on the spot. Terror choked her and she was unable to answer. *Tina didn't believe them.*

'At the bar in The Shard,' said Lukas smoothly.

'She'd practically just got off the plane when I spotted her.'

His confidence allayed her fears. *They could do this.* 'I was dying to see that view of London,' said Ashleigh—which was no lie. 'Then I saw him and forgot all about the view.' *He was a view worth gazing at all on his own.* She looked up at Lukas in what she hoped was besotted admiration. Resisted the temptation to bat her eyelashes. Or to giggle at the thought of what this tough executive would think if she told her that her first view of Lukas had been from his bathtub.

'Me too,' he said. 'I was smitten. We've been together ever since.' *Well done, Lukas.*

Tina's eyes narrowed shrewdly. 'I didn't take you for the "love at first sight" type, Lukas. You struck me as more of a lone wolf. A challenge to the single women of Europe, with your good looks and fortune being quite the prize.'

Lukas froze. Ashleigh gripped her wine glass so tight she thought it would snap.

'Really?' he said. Ashleigh had known him long enough—was it really only twenty-four hours?—to know Lukas was stalling. Immediately, she took over.

She leaned over the table to engage more with Tina. The trouble with dinner for three was the risk of someone feeling excluded. And she didn't want that person to be Lukas's prospective partner in the deal he so badly wanted to close.

'Sometimes it comes when you least expect it, doesn't it?' she said. 'That bolt from the blue, Cupid's arrow, whatever you want to call it. You're not looking for love but it finds you. Then everything else falls away. You just want to be with that one special person. You feel only half alive when you're apart. You live for them.' Her voice trailed away.

Ashleigh had only ever felt that craziness once. She'd broken up with Dan when they'd both graduated from high school and left Bundaberg for different universities. In her first year she'd had a ball, making new friends, dating different guys. Then in second year she'd taken drama as an elective and met Travis. Gorgeous, heartbreaking Travis. They'd been cast in the same production, playing lovers. Travis. The love of her life—in real life as well as on stage. It had been like an addiction—frantic, feverish. Nothing else had mattered except being with him. Not her studies, not her friends. She'd barely scraped through her other subjects. Then the play had ended. No sooner had the audience applause faded than Travis had dumped her.

Now, she realised she was clutching Lukas's hand way too hard. It was a wonder he hadn't yelped at the pressure on it. She released her grip. Thinking back to Travis always brought a rush of pain—even though it had been so long ago.

She looked over to Tina, saw a flash of what looked like regret in her eyes. Tina pursed her unnaturally full lips. 'I remember that feeling,' she said slowly, then briefly closed her eyes as if returning to a happier past. *She's lonely*, Ashleigh thought. 'But it's all stuff and nonsense,' Tina brusquely added, shattering the momentary illusion of vulnerability.

Ashleigh refused to be cowed. 'I don't think it's nonsense at all,' she said. 'I feel like that about Lukas.' She looked up at him, smiling, though she felt her smile was a bit wobbly at the edges. His eyes gave away nothing. 'He feels the same about me, but I don't expect him to say so in public.'

'Uh…no. I'm not good at that kind of stuff,' he said. 'But yes. I… I feel the same.'

His hesitation made it seem more authentic, Ashleigh thought with relief. They hadn't rehearsed anything like this. But it seemed natural to kiss him, her lips pressed lightly against his. She meant the kiss to be brief—mere punctuation to her confession of infatuation for her pretend boyfriend. But Lukas held the kiss, increased the pressure on her mouth until her whole body responded in a wave of dizzying awareness. She broke away, shaken, but determined not to show it. *She should not have enjoyed that so much.* But she had. If she wasn't in a posh restaurant under the narrow-eyed scrutiny of a dragon lady she would not have stopped the kiss.

She looked away from Lukas, not wanting him to see her confusion, and then back to Tina. 'So I guess whether you're a lone wolf like Lukas or a runaway bride like me, you don't know when Cupid's arrow is going to hit and—'

'Just hold it right there,' said Tina, her eyes gleaming. 'You're a runaway bride?'

Why the heck had she brought that up? Lukas's barely audible groan only echoed the groan Ashleigh felt inside. Her salacious bridal history was hardly relevant to Lukas's business deal with Tina.

'You actually bolted from the altar?' said Tina. 'In your wedding gown? I've never known anyone who actually did that.' Was that a sneer or genuine interest from the older woman?

'It wasn't quite that scenario,' said Ashleigh, not daring to look at Lukas. She explained to Tina how she'd cancelled everything just weeks before the wedding then run away to London to escape the flak of being in a town where everyone seemed to know her and Dan and have an opinion about her action.

'Good for you,' said Tina. 'It takes a special kind of guts to do that. Like knowing when to pull out of a business deal your instinct tells you is not going to work. Less messy in the long run.'

Lukas paled under his tan at her words and their possible implication. Ashleigh cursed under her breath. Had her impulsive words ruined the deal for him?

'Does that mean…?' she asked Tina, her eyes imploring the older woman not to blame Lukas for her indiscretion. Tina was obviously used to having power and knew how to wield it.

Tina frowned. 'What? You think I'm referring to my doing business with Lukas? Of course I'm not. I'm still doing due diligence before I come to any final decision.'

Ashleigh couldn't help her sigh of relief. 'I'm so glad to hear that. I…' She was going to say she knew how important the deal was to Lukas but realised that might be construed as showing his hand.

'You're being so supportive, *agápi mou,*' Lukas cut in, as if he had guessed she could be heading towards a blunder.

'And very entertaining,' said Tina. 'A runaway bride! Who knew?'

Ashleigh's mouth felt dry and her heart started pounding. Was Tina mocking her? She had a horrible feeling the older woman was trying to undermine her in front of Lukas. 'You…you wouldn't tell anyone about that, would you?' Ashleigh said. 'I came here to put it behind me.'

'You mean "Billionaire Greek Tycoon Romances Runaway Bride"—that type of headline?' Tina said with gleeful exaggeration.

Ashleigh couldn't help her gasp. All the deception would come out under media scrutiny. She didn't dare look at Lukas. Why, oh, why hadn't she kept her mouth shut?

But Tina continued. 'Trust me, my lips are firmly zipped when it comes to scurrilous gossip. I've been burned by it myself.'

Tina seemed totally genuine. Again pain shadowed her eyes and Ashleigh thought about the nasty divorce Lukas said she had endured. She felt really bad she had called her a cougar. 'Thank you,' she said. But still, she knew she wouldn't be able to relax until the evening was done and her role played out.

Their starters arrived then and it brought a welcome change of conversation. The food was innovative but satisfying with an emphasis on seafood and vegetables. Ashleigh managed a connection with Tina over their shared surprise at how excellent their meals were. Lukas pretended to be offended. Why would they think he would take guests to a restaurant he hadn't first approved? Both she and Tina laughed. But Ashleigh was not surprised when, during the main course, the spotlight shone back on her.

'You're from Australia?' asked Tina. 'I've been to Sydney. Great city.'

'I'm from Bundaberg in Queensland,' said Ashleigh.

'I've not heard of it,' said Tina.

'I guess not many English people would have. Unless you like rum, that is. Bundaberg is famous for its rum. We grow a lot of sugar cane.'

'Your town is famous for rum and sugar? That's kind of fun.'

'It is, isn't it,' said Ashleigh with a grin. She could see how in a different situation, when so much wasn't riding on the outcome, she might enjoy Tina's company.

'You never told me about the rum,' said Lukas.

'You never asked,' she said with a flirtatious tilt of her head.

'What did you do back home, Ashleigh?' asked Tina.

'I managed to evade the family profession of teaching—my parents and my sister are all schoolteachers—and did a degree in accounting. Then somehow ended up managing a flooring company in downtown Bundaberg.' She pulled a face. 'Not very glamorous.'

'The company I run isn't glamorous either,' said Tina. 'Your background would give you an appreciation of a down-to-earth business like retail distribution.'

'Or manufacturing,' said Lukas.

Since when had this turned into a job interview?

'I'd like to hear more about both your businesses, and how they could work together,' Ashleigh said. 'We haven't had a chance to talk much about how your company operates, have we, Lukas?' She climbed her fingers up his chest in flirtatious provocation.

'No,' he said hoarsely.

Tina explained briefly how her father had started their company from small beginnings, then ten years ago had died suddenly and she'd had to step in. She had adored her father; he'd brought her up after her mother had died when she'd been aged ten. 'Fortunately, I'd trailed around the warehouses and transport depots since I'd been a toddler. I knew how it all worked.'

'Tina is being modest,' said Lukas. 'In her time at the helm she's expanded the business beyond anyone's expectations.'

'You took over your parents' company too, didn't you, Lukas, and did much the same thing?' Ashleigh asked.

'Yes,' he said. 'Only Tina's father left a thriving business. Ours was in a horrendous state. No secrets there. It's all a matter of public record.' The way he said *no secrets* made Ashleigh wonder just what secrets he'd buried. It was a shame she wouldn't get a chance to find out. She would be saying goodbye to him in the morning.

She refused to let herself acknowledge the mixed feelings that swept through her at the prospect of that parting. That kiss had aroused a longing for Lukas she had not anticipated. It was going to be very difficult to forget him.

When Ashleigh got up to go to the ladies' room Lukas couldn't help but let his gaze follow the sway of her hips as she made her graceful way to the back of the restaurant. *She was beautiful.*

If he really *had* met her at a bar, he might have been tempted to seduce her. Even in her anorak and simple dress she would have attracted attention.

But tonight there wasn't a trace left of the

scruffy backpacker. She wore her brand new designer clothes with assurance—as if famous labels were all that was in her wardrobe. That confidence gave her a sensual presence that couldn't be purchased in the most expensive shop in Bond Street. It was pure Ashleigh. And along with it came her warmth and charm.

Did she feel his gaze on her? She turned back briefly and smiled at him over her shoulder. Her hair tumbled rich and sleek past her shoulders, rivalling the Christmas decorations with its vivid gleam. Her face was heart-stopping in its love-liness, her eyes expertly made-up to emphasise their extraordinary colour, her mouth lush and naturally pink. *That kiss.* It had taken a monu-mental effort to control himself and not take the kiss deeper, exploring her with lips and tongue. It was only the inappropriateness of a passionate kiss in front of Tina that had stopped him.

'She'll be back in a few moments, you know,' Tina said wryly.

Lukas realised he hadn't heard a word she'd said, too lost in watching Ashleigh. 'I'm sorry,' he said. 'That was unforgivably rude.'

'I notice you haven't taken your eyes off her all

evening and I don't blame you,' she said. 'She's lovely. Beautiful to look at, of course, but also smart and fun.'

'I think so,' he said. His plan had worked out so much better than he had hoped.

'Can you be sure she's not a gold-digger?' Tina said. 'Wealth is a privilege but can also sometimes be a burden. I've been burned a few times by someone I thought was special but was after the money, not me.'

Lukas's first reaction was to tell Tina to mind her own business. But he wanted to work with her. 'She's no gold-digger,' he said. 'Of that I'm certain.'

'You're quite sure?'

'Yes,' he said. He'd met enough of the real deal gold-diggers to be sure Ashleigh was not of their kind.

'Then be careful with her,' Tina said.

Lukas bristled. 'What do you mean?'

'She's a romantic and could be easily hurt.'

'I have no intention of hurting her,' he said through gritted teeth. If he didn't want this partnership with Tina so much he would tell her what he thought of her interference.

Hurt was never going to come into it. His arrangement with Ashleigh was a simple repayment of debt. And when she left tomorrow she would be well ahead of the game. She would take it all with her—the dress, the shoes, even the watch, the value of which she seemed to have no idea. It was quite a haul for one evening's work.

'I hope you mean that,' Tina said, her eyes narrowed. Was this a test? Perhaps she was not as hoodwinked by the charade as he'd thought.

'Of course,' he said.

Hurt could go two ways. So he might feel some regret when Ashleigh walked out of the door. But he'd get over it. Ashleigh was too dangerous for him to be around. She was starting to make him feel things he didn't want to feel. Feelings he'd locked away long ago. Not for her. Not for any woman. Especially not for a runaway bride who'd soon be on her way home to her forgiving fiancé.

He would never fall for that particular story again. That last summer of freedom on Mykonos was when he'd met Céline. They'd spent the season together, only getting out of bed for her to go to work as a waitress and him to crew on a yacht. She'd seemed so different, and he'd let down the barriers he'd erected so early as protection against the cynical arrangements that passed for relationships among his parents and their set. He'd thought it would be for ever for him and Céline. But on the morning she was leaving the island—when he was just about to propose—she'd told him she was going back home to France to the soldier boyfriend she'd told him was off the scene. Lukas's trust had been irrevocably shattered.

Now, he forced his attention away from painful memories and back to Tina.

'I'd like to see you again—and Ashleigh,' she said. 'I have a table for the Butterfly Ball on Friday night. By then I'll have a decision on our potential deal. Can I count on seeing you both there?'

Lukas bit down on his frustration and dismay. This dinner was supposed to be about keeping Tina at arm's length on a personal level. Ashleigh was to be his fake date just for the one night. He'd intended to give a vague answer about her in the unlikely event Tina ever asked after the lovely redhead. Hell, the way he'd planned it, Tina should be jealous of Ashleigh, not wanting to see her again. The sudden change of agenda was unsettling. Ashleigh wouldn't be around by Friday.

At that moment she returned to the table. Her lush mouth was slicked glossy pink, making it look even more kissable. He had to fight the urge to pull her to him and kiss that lipstick right off. Instead he schooled his face to look neutral and stood up to greet her.

'You're back just in time,' he said. 'Tina has invited us as her guests to the Butterfly Ball on Friday night.'

'Oh,' Ashleigh said, obviously as shocked as he'd been. 'Th…that's very nice of you, Tina, but I—'

Tina looked from one to the other. 'I expect to see you both there.' There was steel in his prospective business partner's voice.

Lukas caught Ashleigh's eye, gave a slight nod. He'd noticed they seemed to pick up on the other's slightest variation in body language. She gave him the same signal back to signify her understanding.

'Thank you, Tina, that would be wonderful,' Ashleigh said. 'I was going to say I don't have a suitable dress for a black tie event. But I don't really need an excuse to go shopping in London.'

'Splendid,' the older woman said. She was used to getting her way.

'It's very kind of you to invite us.' Then Ashleigh deliberately wound her slender arms around his neck and looked up into his face. 'Lukas and I have never danced together. This will be a real treat. Won't it, darling?'

He gritted his teeth again. Anger at Tina's manipulation mingled with an overwhelming awareness of Ashleigh's nearness. Did she realise she was playing with fire? He placed his hands around her waist as a good fake boyfriend would. Just what underwear did she have on under that body-hugging dress? The thought had preoccupied him ever since their shopping expedition this morning.

'Yes. A treat,' he said, forcing himself to sound unperturbed by the bombshell Tina had dropped on him.

And even more unperturbed by Ashleigh's curves pressing against his chest.

Ashleigh sensed the tension building in Lukas but he kept it tamped down until after they had said goodnight to Tina outside the restaurant. Tina had declined his offer of a ride in his car, saying she preferred to walk.

Lukas waited until Tina was well out of sight before he slammed his hand against the support of the restaurant portico so hard the force of it must have juddered up his arm. It was lucky it didn't come crashing down on top of them. Thank heaven there weren't any other patrons leaving the restaurant.

He unleashed an impressive stream of what she could only assume were formidable Greek swear words, ending in a very English 'Damn, damn, damn.'

'I'm guessing you're not pleased about the invitation to the Butterfly Ball.'

He glowered dark fury. 'Don't be smart with me, Ashleigh. What do you think? Of course I'm not pleased. This arrangement was supposed to end tonight.'

'But we did well, didn't we? Tina thinks you're taken. You won't have to walk away from your deal because of any embarrassment about Tina wanting more from you than your product distribution agreement.'

'Maybe I imagined her interest in me,' he growled. 'She seems enchanted with *you*.'

'I don't think so. The first thing she felt when she saw me was disappointment. She's lonely. You're hot. You're both rich.'

Lukas grimaced. 'Don't go there. She reminds me of my mother and her friends.' He swore some more, his expression dark.

He was usually so serious, so restrained, so in control. She liked this Lukas, furious he'd been outsmarted. His explosion of dark energy excited her and made her wonder what he'd be like out of control in the bedroom. It was all she could do not to push him up against the wall of the restaurant and kiss him senseless.

Instead he put his hands on the wall behind her. The action brought him very close, effectively trapping her with his body. All this pretend flirting was having an arousing effect on her libido. His dark eyes glittered as he looked down and for the first time she wondered if it might be having the same effect on him.

'So now I'm being coerced into this ball,' he said.

Ashleigh knew he'd shaved before they'd left

for the restaurant yet already there was a dark growth shadowing his jaw. She found it incredibly sexy. What would he do if she reached up and stroked it? She ached to feel its roughness against the smoothness of his olive skin. Better, to feel its roughness against the smoothness of *her* skin.

'You feel you've been manipulated and steamrollered,' she said, fighting for the breath to fuel her words. To force herself to appear unaffected by his closeness, the sense of tightly leashed passion that, if it exploded, might carry her along with its force on a wild ride of sensual discovery.

'After all that, Tina still hasn't come to a decision.' His mouth set in a tight line. What would he do if she teased it open with the tip of her tongue? But he was still obsessed with his business deal. More than likely, he'd still keep on talking about Tina through her kiss.

The passion was obviously staying strictly on its leash. This feeling was pure fantasy on her part. She sighed and directed her thoughts back to where they should be. 'If I can be the voice of reason here, it's still early days. Tina said she still had to complete due diligence. Would you really be interested in a business partnership with a person who took your company evaluation at face detail?'

'Of course not,' he said, his thick dark brows drawn together. Would he look the same in passion as he did in anger?

'Maybe we overdid the lovey-dovey act?' she said. But my, how she'd enjoyed it. He'd given her a taste of what it might be like to go further than that interrupted kiss that had so taken her by surprise.

'Who were you thinking about when you were gushing about being hit by Cupid's arrow?' he growled. 'Your fiancé?'

'I've told you he's my *ex*-fiancé. No. It was someone I fell for when I was too young and naïve to recognise a player for what he was. Not a mistake I ever intend to repeat.'

Ashleigh could sense by his expression he didn't believe her. She shrugged away from him. Stood at a distance with her arms wrapped around her chest. Why should she care?

He shoved his hands deep into the pockets of his overcoat. 'So will you come to the ball with me?'

'You mean more play-acting?'

'If you want to call it that.'

'I don't like the thought of making a fool of Tina. Okay, she's intimidating and I'm not sure she bought our story one hundred per cent. We'd be wise to remain wary of her. But she's not some voracious cougar. I think she's a lonely woman who has suffered a lot of loss in her life.'

He rolled his eyes in an expression of male disgust. 'This is about business, Ashleigh, not bleeding hearts. So the initial plan backfired. Now I realise Tina's one of those managers who likes to interview the partner of any person she plans to work with. And she's taken a shine to you.'

'I took quite a shine to her too. As a fluttery fledgling to her full-grown eagle, that is. If it's so important to you—and I'd like to know why one more deal is so important to you when you're already so wealthy—I'll do it.'

He slumped with relief. 'That's good. I—'

She put up her hand to stop him from going any further. 'On one condition.'

He frowned. 'Condition?'

'I want to stay at your townhouse until after Christmas.'

'You *what*?' The words exploded from him.

'I've got a deal to sleep on my friend's sofa but that's hardly comfortable or convenient for me or Sophie. If you want me to go to that ball and schmooze with scary Tina, that's my price.'

Price mightn't have been the most appropriate word to use. But Lukas was so furious at what he obviously saw as further manipulation he didn't notice the implication. Fact was, she couldn't be bought.

'That's blackmail,' he said.

'And a phony invoice for three nights' accommodation at your house wasn't?'

He glared at her and she glared right back. 'So is it *yes* to letting me stay?'

'Yes,' he said grudgingly.

'And of course you're aware I haven't got anything suitable to wear to a ball?'

'More shopping?' he groaned.

'You don't need to come with me. I've got two days to find something.'

'You can take my credit card. I have one I give to domestic staff for their use in running the household.'

That put her squarely back in her place. 'You

might have to up the limit, considering the prices on Bond Street.'

'Can I trust you—?'

Insult upon insult. 'With your credit card? Are you questioning my honesty?'

He scowled. 'I meant can I trust you to buy something spectacular without worrying about the cost? No penny-pinching. I haven't been to one of these big charity balls for years. You'll have to do me proud.' He looked down at his feet in their handmade Italian shoes. 'Like…like you did tonight.'

Her indignation dissipated like the fog of her breath into the cold night air. 'Thank you. I… I did my best.' It had been surprisingly easy to pretend to be in love with him. To imagine… *No.* It was just business between them and she could not forget that. *Even though he set her heart racing just by his presence.*

'It was a very good best. You handled Tina better than I could have imagined.'

'But you're not happy about me hanging around, are you?'

'You're right about that,' he grunted. 'Tina was

right when she called me a lone wolf. That's the way I like it.'

And wolves could not be tamed. His message could not be any clearer.

They spent the ride to Chelsea in an uncomfortable silence, with Ashleigh squashed against the car door to put as much distance between them as she could. She twisted the strap of her elegant new evening purse so tight it was in danger of snapping as she worried about what she might be getting herself into by living in close proximity to Lukas Christophedes.

Because she had really, really wanted to kiss him into a passionate frenzy against that wall.

CHAPTER EIGHT

THE NEXT DAY, Ashleigh leaned back against her chair in a swish café on the Duke of York Square in Chelsea and subjected herself to her fashion-crazy friend Sophie's scrutiny. She and Sophie had met earlier in the swanky square at the top end of the King's Road. Sophie had been quick to agree to help Ashleigh with a day of shopping for the Butterfly Ball. 'You mean actual shopping in posh shops, as opposed to window shopping?' she'd said. 'Count me in.'

Ashleigh had called in more troops for moral support—Emma and Grace were due to arrive soon. It was a perfect winter's day in London, crisp and clear with a bracing chill. People were talking hopefully of snow.

'You look…different,' Sophie said with a quizzical expression.

'Probably because I'm wearing a few thousand pounds' worth of coat and boots,' Ashleigh said with a laugh. Only the jeans she wore were her own. The black boots, lavender-coloured coat and charcoal top all belonged to Lukas.

Sophie narrowed her eyes. 'It's not just that. Your hair. The make-up.'

'All courtesy of a salon in Mayfair yesterday. They showed me a few tricks that really make a difference. And threw in some samples for me to take home.'

Sophie's eyes widened when Ashleigh named the salon. 'You have got to be kidding. I'd have to take out a mortgage just to have a manicure there.'

'I know. This whole pretend girlfriend thing is surreal. It was like the fairy godmother waved her magic wand over me yesterday. I took a selfie as proof it really happened. Look.'

Ashleigh pulled out her smartphone to show her old friend the snap she had taken of herself in her borrowed finery, just before she and Lukas had left for the restaurant.

Sophie took one look and identified the designer of her dress. 'You look so glamorous,' she said. 'And that fairy dust magic is still lingering. It's difficult to put a finger on it. It's not just the way you look. I think it's a new confidence after all these years of the dreadful Dan undermining you.'

'Maybe. It went well last night. I think I really pulled off the role of billionaire's girlfriend. I kept up with the business talk too. I… I fitted in.'

'Of course you did. You're beautiful and you're a brilliant actress. You were the best by far on the stage in the school productions. But is any of that fairy dust to do with Lukas? Don't tell me you don't fancy him!'

Ashleigh picked up her coffee cup and put it down again. 'Who wouldn't fancy him? He's the handsomest man I've ever met—and *hot*. But I'm just playing a role. So is he.' Not even to Sophie could she admit how much of her thoughts Lukas occupied. Wondering about what it would be like to go on a real date with him. To kiss him for real. To go further than kissing.

'He's not trying to make a move on you?'

Ashleigh shook her head. 'It's strictly business. He's got a real "don't get involved" barrier around him. Which is for the best, really. You know me, a one-night stand isn't my thing. And that's all it would be.' But who knew what might have happened to her scruples last night if that passion she'd felt for him had had a chance to flame?

'Er...of course not,' said Sophie, shifting in her seat.

'It's a tricky situation, but so far I'm managing to keep my cool.'

'Are you sure it's a good idea to be living in his house?'

'I'm perfectly safe there, if that's what you mean.'

'Good. But it sounds like at the moment he really needs you to carry out his plan. Have you thought about afterwards? As soon as that contract is signed he might boot you out.'

'I don't think so,' Ashleigh said slowly. 'My impression is that he's an honourable man in his own way.'

'The offer of my sofa still stands, wonky springs and all,' said Sophie.

Ashleigh smiled at her friend. 'Thank you. It's reassuring to have that safety net. But I know how important it is for you to have your own safe, private place. After what happened with Harry, I mean.'

Sophie put up her hand. 'You know I just want to forget that time in my life.'

But the episode with the Manchester bad boy had scarred her friend, Ashleigh thought. Thanks to email and phone calls, they'd kept their teenage friendship alive. She considered Sophie to be one of her best friends. It had been frustrating to be so far away when Sophie had been in trouble. But they were both in London now, looking out for each other. If Sophie ever needed her, Ashleigh would be here for her. 'I understand, of course,' she said.

'So, on the agenda today is shopping for the role of billionaire's girlfriend for one of the most prestigious events in the London fund-raising calendar,' Sophie said, in an obvious attempt to change the subject. 'And hey, how great you're actually going to a ball as a guest rather than a waitress.'

'I'll be well and truly back to waitressing by the time The Snowflake Ball rolls around on New Year's Eve.'

'I wish there was time for me to make you a gown for tomorrow night,' said Sophie.

'Oh, Sophie, so do I.' Sophie was a talented

designer and preparing to open an online store selling her lovely vintage-inspired designs.

Just then Ashleigh looked up to see Emma and Grace heading towards them from the direction of the Saatchi Gallery. She waved to attract their attention. Then turned back to Sophie. 'Please, don't tell them about the bathtub. You're the only one I'm sharing that particular incident with.'

'And the rest of it?'

'The pretend girlfriend thing? So long as they swear not to say a word to Clio, I'll tell them everything.'

'Clio will find out, you know. She knows everything. Though she seems preoccupied at the moment.'

'Maybe because of that wedding on the weekend. The long-time client who insisted she organise his daughter's wedding—even though she hates weddings, as you know, and isn't actually a wedding planner.'

'Maybe that's it. I'm waitressing at that wedding; are you rostered on?'

'No, thank heavens. Otherwise I would have had to cancel to be free for the Butterfly Ball. And I don't want to mess Clio around.'

'The good news for you is that we're going down to Surrey tomorrow to start setting up for the wedding on Saturday. That means Clio won't be at the Butterfly Ball to spot you with Lukas. You know her rules about dating clients.'

Ashleigh swore under her breath. 'I sure hope the girls are good at keeping secrets.'

Sophie smiled enigmatically. 'Don't worry. We're all very good at that.'

Ashleigh didn't have time to demand an explanation about what secrets Sophie could possibly be keeping when Emma and Grace arrived at the café.

She stood up to greet them in a flurry of cheek kisses and hugs. It wasn't often the four friends were rostered all together on the same jobs for Maids in Chelsea and so they were determined to make the most of this opportunity to catch up in their own time.

Ashleigh had been a little in awe of gorgeous blonde Emma with her posh accent when she'd first met her. But now she couldn't imagine not being friends with her. They'd bonded at a big party where they'd all been waitressing and Emma had panicked at seeing her ex there. Her ex, whom she'd said was her teenage boyfriend but had actually turned out to be her secret teenage husband—the son of a marquess and now the Earl of Redminster in his own right. Their reconciliation had been cause for drama and played out in front of the media. But Emma was really happy now with her beloved Jack. Of course, as the Countess of Redminster, Emma was no longer working as a waitress. But she was the kind of girl who liked to keep her friends close.

'Am I meant to curtsey?' Ashleigh joked as she said hello. 'And do we call you Lady Emma now? Or Lady Redminster? You know we Aussies aren't up on aristocratic etiquette.'

'Of course not,' said Emma in those cut-glass tones. 'No curtseying and I'm just Emma, as I've always been.'

'Have you ordered?' asked Grace. 'I've been looking forward to coffee and cake.'

'Just coffees,' said Ashleigh.

'We were waiting for you guys,' said Sophie.

'Sorry we were a little late,' said Grace. 'You know how much I love Christmas decorations. I was admiring the way the square is decorated.

And there are some fabulous festive knick-knacks in the shops too.'

Ashleigh had found willowy, brown-haired Grace quite shy when she'd first met her but had soon discovered the warm, generous person behind her gentle smile. People had warned her London could be a hostile place—she was so lucky to have made such wonderful new friends here.

'Shall we look at the cake menu?' Ashleigh asked. 'Choose whatever you want. Because morning coffee is on me—or rather on my pretend billionaire boyfriend.'

When the squeals had died down, Emma and Grace demanded to know more.

'We had no idea what to think when you asked us to help you shop for a gown for the Butterfly Ball,' said Emma.

Ashleigh proceeded to give them an edited version of how she came to be Lukas Christophedes's fake date. She left out her presence in his bathtub and her unsettling urge to kiss him last night. She hadn't admitted *that* even to Sophie. 'So I need a ball gown for tonight and Lukas is so relieved he doesn't have to hang around in shops with me he told me to treat my friends to lunch,' she concluded.

'That's great about the lunch,' said Grace. 'What worries me is you having been stranded in the middle of London after the party on Sunday with nowhere to stay,' she added with a frown.

Ashleigh shrugged. 'I was meant to be catching the bus with Sophie but she disappeared on me. What actually *did* happen, Soph?'

'Er… I waited for you at the bus stop then thought you must have made other arrangements,' said Sophie, looking a bit shamefaced, her brown eyes looking down at her coffee cup.

'That's not like you, Sophie,' said Grace.

'I'll let you off the hook this time,' said Ashleigh. But something about Sophie's expression didn't sit right. She'd ask her again later what had happened that night.

'So that means you're definitely not going home to Australia for Christmas?' Emma asked after they'd ordered coffee and a selection of decadent-looking cakes.

'That's right,' Ashleigh said.

'I'm so glad you'll be around in the next few weeks,' said Emma. 'Because—' she paused dramatically '—Jack and I have decided to renew our wedding vows and I want you all to be my bridesmaids.'

Shrieks of delight greeted her announcement but while Ashleigh uttered heartfelt congratulations she remained subdued.

'Are you okay with that, Ashleigh?' asked Emma.

'I'm honoured,' said Ashleigh. 'But we've only known each other a few weeks and I don't want you to think you *have* to ask me because you've asked the others.'

'You should know by now I don't do anything I think I *have* to do. I want you there.' Emma sounded her most imperious countess.

'In that case, I would be delighted to be your bridesmaid,' Ashleigh said, blinking back sudden tears.

'Where are you going to hold the ceremony, Emma?' asked Grace.

'Do you remember we scouted out that funky boutique hotel not far from here, The Daphne?' Emma asked. 'We've booked there.'

'Perfect,' breathed Grace.

Emma turned to Sophie. 'Sophie, I would love

it if you could make my wedding dress—I didn't have one for the "real" wedding. And the bridesmaid dresses, of course. There's you three, and my friend and sister-in-law Clare will be chief bridesmaid.'

'There's nothing I'd love more,' said Sophie. 'But Emma, you could have a top designer. You're a countess. Honestly, I won't be offended if you choose to do that.'

'But I want *you*,' Emma said. 'Not only do I think you'll give me just the look I want, the wedding will give you good exposure too. We want to keep it small and private but we'll have to release some photos to the media. The thing is, the ceremony is six days from today so I know it's a big ask. Jack and I had planned to wait till the new year, but really what's the point? We can't wait to make it official all over again.'

'I can get the dresses done. Even if I have to stay up every night.'

'No need for that,' said Emma. 'We'll need to get you some assistance.'

Ashleigh looked at Sophie and saw the glint of tears in her eyes too. This could be the break her friend needed.

'We should have champagne,' said Grace, her voice also not quite steady.

'There'll be time enough for champagne,' said Emma. 'Right now we need to help Ashleigh find a gown for the Butterfly Ball. King's Road, you said, Ashleigh?'

Ashleigh nodded. King's Road was lined with fabulous shops. She'd been captivated by the windows every time she'd walked by.

'Not so fast,' said Sophie. 'King's Road and here, The Duke of York Square, do have amazing shops. But time is short. I think we need to look at a designer runway collection for Ashleigh's night at a ball with a billionaire. That means changing direction and heading for Sloane Street.'

Ashleigh didn't have a clue what a designer runway collection was, but it sounded exciting—and exclusive. That was what Lukas would want— and she really wanted to play her role for him as best as she possibly could.

It was only a hop and a skip through Sloane Square to Sloane Street—another of London's exclusive shopping streets that ended up in Knightsbridge, home to the posh department stores Harrods and Harvey Nichols.

'I've got the credit card, girls, and I know how to use it,' Ashleigh said. 'Let's finish our coffee and go shopping.'

CHAPTER NINE

LUKAS DIRECTED HIS driver to stop the car outside the imposing entrance to one of London's most famous grand hotels, the venue for the night's Butterfly Ball. The limousine was at the head of a line of chauffeur-driven luxury vehicles and taxis dropping off guests all dressed to the nines in the requisite formal wear.

'Ready?' Lukas asked as he opened Ashleigh's door.

'Shifting right into girlfriend mode as we speak,' she said.

As she emerged from the car he caught his breath at how beautiful she looked. She wore an exquisite silk gown in shades of lavender, topped with a theatrically flamboyant ivory velvet cloak lined with purple. Her hair was piled up on her head with little tendrils escaping to fall down her slender pale neck, purple stones glittered at her ears. *They should be real jewels.* But she could not have chosen anything more perfect for her colouring and for the occasion.

Once more she looked the part he had cast her in, exceeding all expectations with a new level of sophistication and elegance. He could not keep his eyes off her.

'You look magnificent,' he said as he offered her his arm. He ached to say more—so much more—but had to remind himself that they were both playing roles. *It was strictly business.*

'All thanks to your credit card,' she murmured, tucking her hand into his elbow. The action brought her close, so close he could breathe in her sweet scent, feel the warmth of her body. He kept her by his side as they walked into the ornate foyer of the hotel with its show-stopping Christmas tree that soared to the ceiling.

'Thanks also to your good taste,' he said. 'No amount of money can buy that.' Not to mention her innate grace and style—which he'd spotted even when she'd been wearing jeans and trainers. He'd said she should do him proud—and she'd done that in spades.

'You look magnificent yourself,' she said, her dimples flirting in her cheeks. 'Born to wear a tuxedo.' Her compliment pleased him. The women he usually dated were all about accepting compliments—and anything else they could grab from him—rather than bestowing them.

'Nobody is looking at me, I assure you,' he said. 'All eyes are on my beautiful date.'

'I feel like a princess,' she said. 'When I look in the mirror, I can't believe it's me looking back.'

'You outshine any princess,' he said. Did he really say that? He wasn't usually so fulsome. He was rewarded with a display of her dimples.

'I know you're only saying that as part of the act, but thank you,' she said. 'It's just the clothes—you know what they say: clothes maketh the pretend girlfriend.'

He'd meant every word of the compliment. It was an effort to keep the conversation at a superficial level when he found it difficult not to stare at her in admiration. 'You shopped well,' he said.

'I had enthusiastic help,' she said.

It had been the right thing to do but Lukas had regretted letting Ashleigh go out yesterday with her girlfriends instead of him. He could not admit to the time he'd spent imagining her coming out of a fitting room and asking him for his reaction, *What do you think?* Then imagining what it would be like to *show* her what he thought. *He should have been there with her.*

The truth was, he'd missed her. Even though she was now living legally in his house, he hadn't seen much of her. He suspected she'd kept purposefully out of his way and then she'd been at the hairdresser all afternoon. The house had seemed so empty without her.

But these thoughts of missing her, of wanting her, of—God help him—being given the privilege of carrying her parcels, could not be allowed to flourish. She was a beautiful, intriguing woman but what he had with her was just a business arrangement. Besides, she had given no indication that she felt any of the attraction he felt for her. The flirtatious looks, the kisses, the seductive smiles had all been with the aim of impressing Tina Norris—not *him.*

As they waited in the crush of people to get into the ballroom, he took the opportunity to update her on the negotiations with Tina. After all, the deal with Tina was the sole reason they were at the ball.

'Her finance people have talked to my finance people, so I'm hoping the agreement is progressing.'

'What do you want me to do?' she asked.

He had to lean nearer to hear her soft voice over the chatter and hum of hundreds of people. She had divested herself of her cape to leave in the cloakroom and he was tantalisingly close to her smooth, pale arms and shoulders, the swell of her breasts above the strapless dress. *Just like she'd looked in the bubbles.*

He had to clear his throat to speak. 'Just do what you did at our last meeting with Tina. You made such a good impression.'

'It won't be a hardship,' she said. 'I quite like Tina and this hotel is so magical. I feel like I'm in some kind of fairy tale.' Fairy tale to her, concrete business opportunity to him. He wanted it. She could help him get it. That was what all this was about.

As they approached Tina's table near the front of the ballroom, Ashleigh halted him with a hand on his arm. 'Come here,' she said. She made a show of straightening his already perfectly straight bow tie, tweaking it with fingers that feathered over his neck as she did so. It was an intimate caress that only a lover would attempt and, as such, was an inspired gesture on her part. He caught her hand and kissed it, holding the kiss for a beat longer than required. 'Thank you,' he said huskily.

'All part of the job,' she murmured, looking up at him with her wide blue eyes.

Of course that was all it was to her. *And to him.* He was crazy to entertain for one head-spinning moment that it could ever be anything else.

The trouble with a fake date was that you couldn't tell what was real and what was just part of the pretence, Ashleigh thought.

It made it difficult to know just how to respond to Lukas's compliments. He seemed so sincere in his admiration. But then perhaps he was as good an actor as she was. Businessmen of his stature did not get to be where they were without being able to put up a good façade when required, to bluff and feint. She had to stop herself from longing for his admiration to be real.

She was seated by his side as Tina's guests at the older woman's table, Tina to his left, she to his right. The other guests around the circular table were business associates of Tina's, some of whom Lukas was acquainted with. She, of course, knew no one. But she was soon chatting with the other guests. The story about Bundaberg being famous for rum usually went down well.

For a sudden, breath-stealing moment she realised some of the people at this ball might have attended some of the high-end functions where she had worked as a waitress since she'd been in London. 'What if someone here recognises me as their waitress or maid?' she whispered to Lukas.

He snorted his disbelief. 'When you look more beautiful in your finery than the rest of the women here put together?'

'That's patently untrue,' she said with a smile, enjoying the flattery, at the same time wishing it was real.

'I'm entitled to my opinion,' he said, which made her smile deepen. Then he had to go and remind her of the gulf between them by adding, 'Besides, who *ever* notices the help?'

'I guess not,' she said, her voice trailing away. *Unless he finds them naked in his bathtub.*

She looked around her, admiring the splendour

of the ballroom with its period style glamour. The room was elaborate yet elegant with panelled walls, ornate ceiling and outsized chandeliers all in the style of a bygone era. The hotel sat on the north bank of the Thames and the windows revealed a splendid view of the river. She felt entranced by the myriad lights of the city she was growing to love, the iconic London Eye slowly revolving through the dark.

It made her remember Emma's glow when she'd told them how Jack had taken her up on the Eye to toast her with champagne at midnight. Emma had gone through hardship and humiliation to get to the happy place she was now, yet Ashleigh could not help a twinge of envy.

She had got engaged to Dan for all the wrong reasons and ended the engagement for all the right ones. Yet for all her brave move in running away, for all her words about independence, deep down she longed for love with the right man one day. But here she was in the most cynical of sham relationships with the only man she'd found attractive since she'd arrived in London.

But it was difficult to feel maudlin in Tina's down-to-earth company. 'We're here to help support this wonderful charity,' she said. The charity funded research into premature and stillbirths. 'But we're also here to enjoy a Christmas get-together,' the older woman said. 'Let's eat, drink and be merry.'

It was a good deal more than that, as far as Lukas was concerned, and Tina knew it. But who was Ashleigh to question her reason for being here at such a glamorous occasion in the most beautiful dress she had ever worn? And—if the look in Lukas's eyes was genuine—a dress in which she looked her best.

Her shopping expedition in Sloane Street had been beyond her wildest expectations. As soon as the sales associate—giving awesome service with a countess as part of the party—helped her slip into the designer gown, Ashleigh had known it was the one.

'This is the dress,' Sophie had said, echoing her thoughts.

Ashleigh had been grateful for her friends' presence to help her shop. But she had felt a moment of wrenching disappointment there was no tall, dark-haired man waiting outside for her to watch her twirl the skirts around and ask, *What do you think?* She'd missed him. Looking back on that wonderful day in Bond Street, much of the magic had come from being with Lukas. And it was nothing to do with him being a credit-card-wielding billionaire—it was Lukas the man she was so unwisely growing attached to.

At the same shop she had found delicate shoes in purple suede, high-heeled, that wrapped around her ankles with soft suede ties. Pinprick-sized diamanté were scattered over the suede. Then they'd found outsize teardrop-shaped ear-rings that went perfectly with the dress and the faux amethyst bracelet.

No wonder she felt like a princess. And she was determined to enjoy every moment of this eve-ning with the man more darkly handsome than any prince. Even if under ordinary circumstances he would never have noticed her. She refused to admit how much that hurt.

Lukas tried not to look bored as he sat through the inevitable talks about the good work of the charity and the speeches from its patrons. He pledged a hefty donation to the appeal. He re-frained from pressing Tina for a decision—that would be poor form at a social occasion. And he begrudged the amount of time Ashleigh spent chatting with the other people at the table. Especially the men. It was irrational, he knew, but he wanted her to himself. She was *his* pretend girlfriend.

After the main course had finished, a show dance by professional ballroom dancers was announced. The dancers were stars of a popular television dance show and there was much applause.

The male dancer, slender and dark, and his partner in a flame-coloured spangled dress drew gasps from their audience with their skill. Lukas could see Ashleigh was entranced. She watched the dancers' every move, swaying to the rhythm of the music, tapping her feet. Lukas, in turn, watched her. He should warn her that her obvious interest would make her a target for when the dancers selected someone from the audience to dance with them. Ashleigh, with her beauty and enthusiasm, was a prime target. And if she danced like she sang… He would hate to see her humiliated.

But, before Lukas could say anything, the male

dancer was by Ashleigh's side. She protested, saying her dress wasn't right but if he insisted she would love to dance with him. He took her by both hands and drew her to her feet. Flushed and laughing, she turned her head to Lukas. He nodded. She didn't need his permission. 'Good luck,' he said as she was led away by the handsome dancer.

Tina turned to Lukas. 'Don't look so woeful; he won't steal your lady away.'

His lady.

Ashleigh was *not* his lady. She had a man back in Australia—not for a moment did Lukas believe she wouldn't reconcile with him. Besides, he hadn't changed his mind about commitment. He liked his life exactly the way it was. His mansion in Athens. His townhouse in Chelsea. The private Ionian island that had belonged to his grandmother and now belonged to him.

He had the freedom to come and go as he pleased without answering to anyone. Sailing in summer. Skiing in winter. Women when it suited him. The type of women who knew the score and made no demands—if they did, he disentangled himself immediately. Once the women got his gift of jewellery they knew it was over.

He didn't date women like Ashleigh Murphy.

Not that he'd ever met a woman quite like her. She was unique. Special. At the spontaneous burst of applause Lukas sat up straighter in his seat and stared, astounded. *And she was a fabulous dancer.*

Ashleigh was not at the level of the polished professional but she was not far from it. Her partner stepped her into a sweet, simple waltz, slowly gliding Ashleigh around the floor. She gracefully dipped and swayed with utter confidence, her skirts swirling around her, revealing her slender, strong legs. *Dancer's legs.*

Lukas could see the astonishment on the professional's face. Then, after a murmured consultation with Ashleigh and a signal to the band, the music completely changed tempo to a sensual Latin rhythm. Ashleigh tossed back her head— haughty, sensuous—slowly entwined her fingers with her partner's and launched into a sinuous, sensual tango. This was a different Ashleigh, accomplished, confident, radiating sensuality and passion—the backpacker banished for ever. Lukas could not keep his eyes from her.

It was just a dance. But while Lukas joined Tina and the other guests in murmurs of amazed admiration, under the table his hands clenched into fists at the sight of Ashleigh in another man's arms. He wanted to wrench the man's hands from where they splayed against her bare skin. Even though common sense kept reminding him it was just a dance.

The performance was no longer about the expert toting the amateur around the room as entertainment. This had become another show dance—a showcase for the talent and skill of his pretend girlfriend. Her hair gleamed copperbright under the lights, her pale skin and pastel dress in contrast to the black trousers and shirt of her dance partner. Tiny lights twinkled from her shoes, her feet in constant motion.

Ashleigh put emotion as well as skill into the dance that was once banned for its blatant sexuality. Her lips were parted seductively, her eyes gleamed with passion and desire, her hips swayed in invitation as she danced. Lukas saw a stranger at the same time he saw sweet, funny Ashleigh.

A sensuous, beautiful woman with a life quite separate to his: not his maid, not his fake date, rather a woman with her own agenda. An exciting woman.

He wanted her. Lukas wanted her so much he ached. He would deny it to her. Deny it to anyone else. But he could no longer deny it to himself.

The vertical expression of a horizontal desire—that was what Lukas's mother used to call the tango after she'd had one too many flutes of champagne at those parties that used to fill his parents' house. Only now did he understand what she'd meant.

He knew Ashleigh had no interest in the other man. It was all about the performance. But she made her passion for her partner disconcertingly believable. He realised what a skilled actor she was—how much could he believe of how she reacted to *him*?

She ended the dance bent backwards over her partner's leg in a symbolic gesture of sensual surrender. Then the dancer swept her to her feet and waltzed around with her as the guests were invited onto the dance floor.

Lukas didn't wait around for pleasantries at his

table. He had to get to Ashleigh before any other man claimed her as a partner. Within seconds he was at her side as she thanked the professional with a hug. He heard her talking to him about a dance school in east London as the guy departed.

For a moment Ashleigh was stranded on the dance floor, alone and uncertain. Lukas could see her hesitate about what to do next. She was a newcomer to London, surrounded by a sea of strangers. He felt an unfamiliar surge of protectiveness towards her.

'Ashleigh,' he called, staking his claim.

She turned and her face seemed to light up in delight as she caught sight of him. 'Lukas!' He smiled with pleasure at her reaction, then reminded himself how skilled she was at playing a role. 'Did you see us?' she asked a little breathlessly. 'I adore the tango. The dress held me back a bit—I should have been wearing something shorter and slinkier.'

Lukas had to close his eyes against the image of her body on display in something *shorter and slinkier.*

'You were incredible.' He took her arm, making it known to the entire room of people that she was *his*. 'The next dance is mine,' he said with a fierce surge of possessiveness.

Her eyes widened. 'Of course it is. I'm yours.' Words spoken in character as his make-believe girlfriend. Yet he responded to them with something visceral from a place deep inside his soul that he had repressed for so long he'd denied it existed. *He wanted to make her his.*

Her face was flushed, her eyes bright, more of her hair had escaped from its confines to tumble around her neck. *Like she would look after passionate lovemaking.*

'Why didn't the fact you were a professional dancer come into our get-to-know-you sessions?'

'You didn't ask,' she said with a provocative tilt to her head.

'So it was your secret?' He realised how little he really knew about her. How much he wanted to know. How many other secrets did she hold?

'No secret. It just didn't seem relevant. I studied dance as soon as I could walk. Ballet. Tap. Jazz. Then ballroom. I'm qualified to teach. I thought about going professional at one stage.'

'What stopped you?'

'Injury. My right knee.' She looked down towards her leg without seeming to realise she did it, held out her foot in its twinkling purple shoe. 'I'll pay for this tomorrow—my knee will be swollen and throbbing. But it was worth it. To dance with such a skilled partner in this beautiful room.'

They were now standing in the midst of other people dancing around them, accidentally bumping into them, apologising in the way English people did, even when they were not at fault.

'Shall we dance?' he said, holding up his hands to her.

Her eyes lit up. Was that genuine delight at the prospect of dancing with him? Or part of the act? Without hesitation she put one hand in his and placed the other on his shoulder. 'With pleasure,' she said.

He swung her into the waltz. Immediately, she followed his lead as they fell into the rhythm of the dance. He was intensely aware of her closeness, her hand clasped in his own much bigger one, his other hand resting on the small of her back. *It was as intimate as a kiss.*

'Hey, you didn't tell me you could dance,' she said. 'You're very good.'

'My parents considered learning to dance part of my education.'

'Do you do traditional Greek dancing?' she asked as he whirled her around. She was so adept at the waltz it was obvious she didn't even have to think about what steps she took.

'But of course. Many Greek men enjoy *horos*. Dance is part of our traditional celebrations.' He realised he hadn't taken part in the traditional dances he'd enjoyed so much for a long time—rarely since his time on the islands when a day's sailing had ended in a *taverna* where all the men had joined in the dance, much to the delight of the tourists. He'd thought onc day he would pass on the traditional dances of his ancestors' islands to his son—a dream long locked away.

His dreams and hopes had been frozen that night of the incident with his mother's friend, when he'd realised his parents cared too much for their decadent lifestyle to protect their son from the lascivious gazes of their guests—men as well as women. Up until then, he'd still sought their approval. But the scales had fallen from his eyes that night. He'd put a lock on his bedroom door and on his emotions.

The waltz came to an end and the music changed to a jazzy quickstep. The dance was energetic and lively and he swung Ashleigh into it, gliding and hopping where required. 'You really know how to dance,' she said, almost accusingly, as if he'd withheld such vital information from her. 'This is such fun.'

Fun. She'd accused him of putting work over enjoying life. Since when had work become an obsession, a shield? Having fun with her was opening chinks in that shield and he wasn't sure how he felt about it.

At the end of the dance she collapsed against him, relaxed, uninhibited, laughing. She was all soft curves and warmth. He felt exhilarated by the energy of the dance, by her nearness, and he joined in her laughter. He realised he had laughed more in the days since he'd met Ashleigh than he had for a very long time.

His dancing teacher at school had berated him for his mechanical correctness in his dancing. 'It's not enough to get the steps right,' she'd said. 'You have to *feel* the dance.'

Dancing with Ashleigh, he finally felt it.

'What's next? Foxtrot? Cha-cha? Bring it on,' he said.

She looked up at him with a quizzical expression, her eyes still warm with laughter. 'You're full of surprises, Lukas Christophedes—and I'm enjoying discovering them.'

Did she mean that? Or was it all part of the act? He realised how much he wanted her to mean it.

Then the music changed to something slow and smoochy and contemporary. The kind of music that didn't call for steps but a sensual swaying, a pressing of bodies close to each other—a couple's dance.

Ashleigh took a step back from him. For a long moment his gaze locked with hers. Traces of laughter lingered in her eyes, to be replaced by something moodier that seemed to be an echo of the want that coursed through him. She wound her arms around his neck and pulled him close—breast to chest, thigh to thigh—in what was sanctioned as a dance but felt more like an intimate embrace, a prelude to a passionate kiss. He captured her thigh between his legs and they moved slowly together. *Did she want to be closer as much as he did?*

* * *

Lukas. Ashleigh gave herself over to his embrace, his arms holding her tight, his strong body pressed as close as her full skirts allowed. She ached for him to kiss her. Ached for so much *more* than a kiss. She wanted him badly. So badly she might make an utter fool of herself if he didn't feel the same. She thought she'd seen a new light in his dark eyes, a recognition of desire, a *connection.* But was it just part of the fake date— a touch of passion to add authenticity? She had never felt more uncertain of a man.

But dancing with Lukas, the waltz, felt so right—their rhythms so in step. She gasped out loud at the thought of how it might be if they became lovers. Lukas pulled away from her. 'You okay?'

'F...fine,' she stuttered. He seemed so calm, unaffected by this intimate dance—while she was a quivering wreck of want. Had she misread him entirely?

Over his shoulder, she noticed Tina making her way towards them. Ashleigh edged closer to Lukas, pressed her lips near his ear in what would surely look like a kiss to Tina. 'Tina alert—better look convincing.' Back to work on her role as a loving girlfriend—which was becoming more and more difficult as she started to want it to be for real.

But, instead of holding her tighter, Lukas stiffened, disengaged himself from her arms and abruptly stepped back from her. 'You're right to remind me. I should ask Tina to dance,' he said gruffly without looking at her.

Baffled and shaky, Ashleigh pasted a smile on her face and watched him walk away. She was still warm from the heat of his body but was rapidly cooling. Of course it was all still about the game for him. All about business. It would all be over tomorrow. She'd been a fool to even imagine it could be anything more. But he had aroused a tumult of feelings and desires in her that would not easily dissipate. *She would not let him see how it hurt.*

While Lukas danced with Tina, Ashleigh danced with Tina's business associate and made polite small talk with a huge effort. Then she danced with Tina's other guest while Lukas danced with the guest's wife. But even while Ashleigh did her duty dances her eyes were on

Lukas, hungry for any glimpse of his sternly handsome face, his surprisingly graceful body. She only danced with him once again, at arm's length. She looked up at him and smiled so much the corners of her mouth ached. Pretend girl-friend was all he wanted—and she would continue to put on the best act she could. She would not give him any hint of her growing feelings. It would only embarrass both of them.

All pretence of a relationship was dropped after the ball was over and Lukas's driver drove them back to Chelsea. It became so awkward and un-comfortable that Ashleigh slumped back against her seat and pretended to be asleep.

She didn't think she fooled Lukas one little bit.

CHAPTER TEN

WHEN ASHLEIGH AWOKE next morning, Lukas's townhouse seemed very quiet. She lay back against the pillows and listened to the sounds of the house—the clock ticking, the slight shifting of old timbers, the occasional clank from the central heating. But there were none of the muted footsteps, the doors shutting, his muffled voice on the phone in the distance that she associated with the master of the house being in residence.

He must be out at one of his meetings, perhaps even with Tina Norris while his prospective business partner was still in town. Good. Ashleigh would find it hard to be chirpy and upbeat this morning. Unusually for her, she felt down, even a touch depressed. This was how Cinderella must have felt when her carriage turned back into a pumpkin and her footmen into mice. Oh, and her touched-by-fairy-dust wardrobe shrivelled back into a hand-me-down anorak and jeans.

The glorious lavender ball gown hung outside the closet where she'd left it to air last night. It looked like a work of art. The shoes had been kicked off haphazardly when she'd staggered into the room, her feet protesting against so much dancing in new leather. Those shoes! Of all the wonderful clothes Lukas had bought to outfit her for her role as pretend girlfriend, the purple suede shoes were the one thing she wished she could afford to buy from him to take with her when she left.

All around her London was fizzing with Christmas spirit. She felt like a balloon that had lost all its gas.

Fact was, Lukas had no further use for her. If Tina signed the deal—and all indications had looked good last night—the pretend girlfriend could be shunted backstage. And maybe onward to Sophie's sofa. Their paths were unlikely to cross again and she felt immeasurably sad about it. She'd become hyper-sensitive to his mood. He'd already started to distance himself from her, if the way last night's ball had ended was any indication.

Ashleigh swung her legs out of bed. Felt a

twinge of discomfort from her right knee—no more dancing for a while. There was a fluffy white bathrobe in the closet that she'd been wearing, thoughtfully left there for guests. She slipped into the robe and a pair of multi-striped socks and headed downstairs.

As she neared the basement kitchen the aroma of coffee reached her. A step closer and she heard the hiss of steam from the coffee machine. When she stood at the threshold she saw Lukas. He sat at the table with his broad back to her, his laptop open in front of him and a mug of coffee nearby. He was wearing a dressing gown too, thick velour in a geometric pattern of burnt orange and chocolate brown. It came to his knees and his legs were bare—strong, tanned with just the right amount of dark hair.

From somewhere—*not her heart...surely not her heart*—came the fierce urge to loop her arms around him from behind, to nuzzle into his neck, drop a kiss there and say how wonderful the ball had been last night. How much she'd loved dancing with him. How awesome he'd been. As if he really was her man. But she couldn't do that. And she couldn't mention the ball. Because then she would have to acknowledge the feelings he'd aroused in her as he'd danced her around the room in his arms.

Ashleigh paused, uncertain whether or not to creep back up the stairs and stay out of his way. But she wasn't a person to run away from an uncomfortable situation—the exception being her ill-fated wedding.

She remembered the excruciating silence in the car on the ride home from the ball, the stilted 'goodnight's when they'd got back here. The refusal on either side to acknowledge the sizzle of attraction between them that had burned up that dance floor. Or had the way he'd held her, the hunger in his eyes been all part of the game of pretend?

'Good morning,' she said, attempting chirpy but resulting in croaky. 'Any chance of a coffee?'

'Of course,' he said. He went to get up. She caught her breath at how handsome he looked, his jaw shadowed with dark growth, his hair unruly and falling over his forehead. Of course it wasn't her *heart* that reacted to him—it was her body thrilling to the sight of him, remembering last night and the erotic sensation of the dance. *It was her body wanting him, not her heart.*

'Stay there. I can make my own.'

She prepared the coffee in silence. Then sat down two chairs away from him, nursing her mug in her hands. 'I didn't expect to find you here. Thought you'd be gone off to a meeting.'

'It's Saturday,' he responded, with more of a grunt than words. Did he have a hangover? She hadn't seen him drink more than a few glasses of wine.

'Oh. Of course,' she said. The last days seemed to have merged into each other with that feeling of a life that wasn't quite real.

'Lukas?'

'Yes,' he said, barely looking up.

'If it's Saturday, why are you working?'

Finally, he took his eyes from the screen. The dressing gown had fallen open to reveal rather more sculpted male chest than she felt able to deal with right now. She flushed and forced her eyes away as she remembered how good it had felt to be crushed against him while they were dancing. He had felt it too, she'd convinced herself. But she'd obviously been wrong—very wrong.

Too late she realised how intimate it seemed now, both of them in their dressing gowns drinking coffee. She should have gone back upstairs and changed. She had boxer shorts and a T-shirt under her dressing gown. His legs were bare, his chest was bare. What else was he wearing—or not?

'Because I'm *always* working. Anyway, how do you know I'm working? I could be playing chess or reading the newspaper online.'

'You could be, but you're frowning so deeply it could only be work. What is it? A problem with the Tina deal?'

His frown deepened into a scowl. 'Running a business like mine means problem-solving twenty-four-seven.'

'That doesn't leave much room for *life*.'

'My work is my life; I've told you that. Every day is a work day for me.'

'Even at Christmas?'

'Why not? Christmas Day is just like any other day to me.'

She gasped. 'You can't mean that.' His words would have counted as heresy in her family.

'I most certainly do.'

'I didn't take you for a Scrooge.'

'Humph,' he muttered.

'Actually, that grumpy noise did sound a lot like Scrooge. Though a *bah, humbug* would have been better.'

The ghost of a smile lightened his scowl. 'You will not get me to say *bah, humbug.* Christmas is as big a deal in Greece as it is here. But not for me. My parents weren't religious and Christmas was just another excuse for a round of parties. They gave the lavish presents, but there was never any real feeling in it.'

'That's such a shame. Even when you were a little boy?'

'My English nanny did her best but she always went home for Christmas. I used to beg her to take me. One year my parents let me go with her and—'

'They let their little boy go to a different country to stay with strangers?' She didn't try to disguise her shock.

He made the *humph* noise again. 'My parents were the strangers. My nanny was more family to me than they ever were. They wanted to go on a cruise where a little boy would have been an inconvenience. That Christmas in her family's very ordinary house in a suburb of Birmingham was the best I ever had. I still remember it. Sadly, never to be repeated.'

Ashleigh felt stunned by the image of the lonely little boy with dark hair and unhappy brown eyes, unwanted by his family at Christmas. But she knew Lukas would not respond well to pity. 'My family has always made a big deal about Christmas. The tree. The presents. The dinner. Because my father is English, we always have the full-on traditional meal with all the trimmings—even in the sweltering heat of a Queensland summer.'

'Christmas in summer? It doesn't seem right.'

'It doesn't really, does it? The two winter Christmases we spent in Manchester were magic. But there's something to be said for a hot Christmas too. My family has a swimming pool and some years we'd take our food outside and eat in the pool.'

'You sound very close to your family.' There was a note of wistfulness in his voice that grabbed at her heart.

'I am.'

'So why are you staying in London and not going home?'

Why would she go into detail about Dan's infiltration of her family—and their disloyalty to her in encouraging it? Lukas wouldn't want to hear all that; he'd probably find it boring. She'd give the easy answer. 'Because I want to enjoy the full English Christmas experience. I'm just hoping it's going to snow.'

'It doesn't often snow in London for Christmas.' His voice was blunt, negative. Had his unhappy childhood squeezed out all the joy of Christmas? Now she felt sad, not just for the little boy but also for the adult Lukas. He deserved so much more. She wished she could be the person to give him the happiness and joy that would lift those dark shadows.

'Well, I hope it will for me.' She got up from the table. 'Can I make you some breakfast?'

'No, thank you.' He pointed to the coffee. 'That's all I want.' Everything he said, the way he kept his gaze on his screen, indicated he didn't want more from her than their agreed upon charade. She should probably grab something from the fridge and take it back to her room. But her hours with Lukas were limited and she was not going to squander them—no matter his not so subtle message of *leave me alone*.

'I'll make toast for me.'

'The toaster is—' He paused. 'I forgot. You know your way around the kitchen. Probably better than I do.'

'Uh…yes.' She still cringed at any reminder of her misdemeanour.

'About that. The day you were out shopping, I contacted Clio at Maids in Chelsea and told her I needed your maid service full-time while I was in residence.'

'You did? I haven't had a chance to do much housework while I—'

'I didn't expect you to. You've been working for me in a different way. But Clio won't be booking you for other assignments. Saves any messy explanations about what you're doing here.'

'Thank you,' she said. She paused for a long moment—too long as it began to feel uncomfortable. 'I know I'm here in your house under sufferance.'

He didn't disagree.

'And I'll stay out of your way as much as I can.

Christmas Day is next Friday. I'm a bridesmaid for a wedding on Wednesday. Well, it's really a renewal of vows. My friend got married in secret when she was eighteen and didn't have a proper wedding. But now—'

He made an impatient wave of his hand. 'Okay. I get it.' Then, seeming to realise how abrupt— even rude—he'd sounded, he said, 'I'm sorry. Weddings hold no interest for me.'

His words came back to her: *I never will marry.* He was happy to be labelled a *lone wolf.* What was the point of even imagining there could ever be anything between them?

'Okay,' she said through gritted teeth. 'No wedding talk. But I'll be out all day tomorrow doing bridesmaid duty.'

He nodded. 'Okay.'

'Any word from Tina?'

His deal with Tina was his only interest in her. Of course he didn't want to hear about her friend's ceremony—even if the bride was a countess and married to an earl. She was dying to tell someone about being Emma's bridesmaid. But she couldn't even call her best friend back in Bundaberg as she was yet another person annoyed with her for walking out on the wedding.

Lukas shook his head. 'Tina doesn't work on weekends if she can avoid it, she says.'

'Like sensible people,' Ashleigh said pointedly.

He did the *humph* thing again.

'So I'm still playing my girlfriend role?'

'Until I tell you otherwise,' he said.

The kitchen ended in a wall of French windows looking out onto the garden. 'Look at the beautiful day out there,' she said, indicating the garden. 'I'm told those clear blue skies aren't the norm for London at this time of year. As your official pretend girlfriend, I suggest you get outside and enjoy this crisp winter day instead of working all the time.'

'That's beyond the scope of your role,' he growled.

She took a deep steadying breath. 'Lukas, look at me, please.'

Grudgingly, he raised his head from his laptop. His dark brown eyes didn't give anything away.

'We get on well, don't we?' she said. 'Perhaps it's only the pretend versions of ourselves that get on but I've enjoyed the time I've spent with you.

In spite of…of an awkward beginning. And unless you're such a good actor you should be playing in the West End, I don't think you've found my company objectionable.'

It certainly hadn't seemed that way on the dance floor.

He frowned. 'Where are you going with this?'

'I'm finding this…awkward. Couldn't we actually pretend to be friends in the time we have left in each other's company? I mean, just between you and me. When we're anywhere in public we can keep up the boyfriend/girlfriend thing until the deal with Tina is finalised. But when it's just us, do we need to put barriers up? It's the festive season. Each of us is on our own. London must surely be one of the most magical places in the world to be for Christmas. Can we enjoy some of it together? As…as friends?'

She knew she wanted so much more than that from him. It would be like a scrap thrown from the master's table but at the moment she just wanted to grab any time with him—no matter the circumstances.

Lukas stared at her for such a long moment she started to shift from foot to foot in her crazy striped socks. He could see regret dim the astonishing blue of her eyes. Regret and *rejection*. He didn't want her to feel that kind of pain.

He was being boorish to her. She didn't deserve that just because he'd woken up irritable and out of sorts after a bad night's sleep. Just because she'd made it clear last night that the surprising intimacy of the dance had just been part of the game he'd staged between them to fool Tina. When he'd found himself wanting so much more.

Those exhilarating moments when he'd been dancing with her, he'd been convinced she'd felt it too—the feeling that was infiltrating in a matter of a few days the barriers he'd erected years ago around his emotions. But then she'd brought him crashing back to reality with her murmured reminder that they'd better *look convincing*. He'd known this woman for such a short time but it had gone way beyond a game for him. He should brush her off. Protect himself. But he could not pass up the opportunity to spend more time with her.

'Friends? Great idea.' He forced enthusiasm into his voice, and was rewarded with a sighting of her dimples.

'You mean that?'

She was offering him something *real*. Not pretend. He doubted she was capable of fake friendship. But how could he be *friends* with a woman for whom he felt such an intense attraction?

'What do you suggest that *friends* might do on a day like this?' he said gruffly. He knew what he'd like to do, but imagining her naked with him in his bedroom, her back in his bathtub this time with him, went beyond any platonic concept of friendship.

'Do you need to buy any gifts? It's the last Saturday before Christmas; the shops—' Her cheerful, practical voice put paid to any lingering thoughts that she might share any of the same sensual fantasies.

'My personal assistant in Athens has organised all that.'

'Even for your family?'

'Yes,' he said, tight-lipped. 'She knows my family's tastes better than I do.'

'That seems so...impersonal.'

'But efficient.'

'Whatever works for you,' she said. Was there implied criticism there? If so, he didn't bite.

Christmas with his parents was impersonal

and soulless and left him feeling sad. The last few years had been particularly depressing. Once he'd hit thirty there were constant hints from his parents that it was time for him to settle down— they wanted children in the house for Christmas. It seemed as they'd aged they had turned to traditional family life but he couldn't believe they were sincere. The scars from their neglect ran too deep. Even though his mother had gone into rehab for her drinking, apologised for her neglect, expressed her horror at the incident with her former friend. That was why he'd decided to spend Christmas this year in Chelsea. Being on his own couldn't be worse than being lonely in the company of other people.

'It works,' he said dismissively. He'd already revealed too much to Ashleigh. She was turning his long-established life of avoiding emotional commitment upside down with unwarranted hopes and longings. Not only did she still have a man in Australia but she'd also stated she wanted to stay single.

Could he entice her into a no-strings affair? He immediately dismissed the idea. Not just because she was not the type for casual and carnal but neither was *he*. Not with this woman. The realisation shook him to his very core. *It terrified him*.

Ashleigh went on, determinedly cheerful. He was so shaken he barely heard her. 'What about Christmas decorations? Do you have any packed away here? Maybe in the attic?'

'No. I've never spent Christmas in this house. I always spend it in Athens.'

'It's a shame not to have at least a tree in this fabulous house. There's a Christmas market in the King's Road today. I'm sure they would have decorations and—'

'Too crowded. The shops will be packed. If you want decorations buy them at Harrods during the week and have them delivered. You still have the credit card I gave you, I assume?'

She snatched her hand to her mouth. 'I'm sorry. I forgot to give it back. But I assure you I haven't used it since—'

'I meant you to keep it. Until after…after—' Whatever he said would sound offensive.

'Until I'm no longer useful to you.' Her eyes dimmed and her mouth turned down.

'I didn't mean—' He hated the look of hurt on

her face but struggled to find the words to suggest there could be a different direction for them.

She put up her hand to halt him. 'Of course you did and it doesn't matter. I know the score. I never assumed—'

She was right. She didn't assume, she didn't take advantage. And she wanted to be *friends*. For the few days she would spend in this house before she went back to her own world, so very different to his. How could he have imagined, even for a fleeting moment, that it could be any different?

'You made an excellent impression on Tina. Anything you spent on the credit card was worth it. If you want to buy Christmas decorations just do it.'

'Thank you, I will. The house doesn't feel festive without at least a wreath at the front door.'

'Or a pomegranate hung there.'

'A pomegranate? Is that a Greek custom?'

'For good luck,' he said.

Ashleigh smiled. 'We might have to settle for an English wreath,' she said.

We. They were not a couple. They would never be a couple. So why did it send such a warm feeling through him when she referred to them as *we*? Ashleigh Murphy was turning everything he'd been so sure of completely upside down.

He closed the lid of his laptop. There were no problems there that couldn't be solved at a later time. 'Perhaps you're right. I should go out with my friend. Where do you want to go? Apart from shopping, that is?'

'Seriously?'

He nodded.

'I want to go ice-skating at the Natural History Museum.'

CHAPTER ELEVEN

ICE-SKATING WASN'T AS easy as she had imagined, Ashleigh thought, as she slid and slipped on the ice while other skaters whizzed by her to the sound of recorded Christmas carols. She had visited the Natural History Museum in South Kensington for the first time as a teenager when she'd been living in Manchester and been enthralled by its displays of dinosaurs and whales. When she'd heard there was an outdoor ice rink set up in the grounds of the museum during winter she'd put it on her wish list for when she was in London.

It didn't disappoint. While she and Lukas waited for their session to start she'd been mesmerised by the beauty of the imposing Victorian buildings of the museum reflected in the ice, surrounded by winter-bare trees and a towering Christmas tree. However, her skills on ice were a definite disappointment.

'Why didn't you tell me this was your first

time skating?' said Lukas. But he seemed more amused than angry as he steadied her with his arm around her.

'I'm a dancer, I've skied—I thought it would be easy.'

'It is, once you get the hang of it.'

'Then what am I doing wrong?' she yelped, as her right foot went the opposite way she wanted it to. 'I'm just not getting it.'

'Bend your knees, use the edges of your blades, lean forward and don't look down—I said don't look… Ashleigh, don't look—' *Oomph*. His words were lost in a gasp of expelled air as she came down on the ice, pulling him down with her. 'Protect your fingers from other peoples' blades—make a fist,' he said urgently.

Ashleigh had come down hard and was too winded to reply. 'Sorry,' she finally gasped.

'Let's get you off the ice,' he said, hooking his arms under hers and hauling them both back upright. That was where her balance and strength did help her get back on her feet. 'Come on, we'll take to the side, where you're out of the way.'

'So sorry,' she said. He was so accomplished, so confident and she felt foolish he was having to help her. But she loved his protectiveness, his strength, the sure way he held her. *Lap it up, Ashleigh, enjoy being friends.*

'Stop apologising,' he said. 'You're a learner. You fell. No big deal. You're wearing hired skates too, which are not ideal.' He, of course, had his own skates.

She leaned in relief against the low wall that enclosed the rink. 'Thank you.'

'Ready to go again?' he said.

'Sure.' She put weight on her right foot and winced.

'Something hurting?' She was surprised at the concern in his voice.

'My knee. This wasn't the brightest idea I've ever had. Not after all the dancing last night. I should have put ice on my knee, not put my knee on the ice.'

He put his arm around her shoulder and she leaned back against its strength and comfort. That made it almost worth crash-landing on the ice.

'It's a shame,' he said. 'You were doing well.'

'No need to be kind,' she said with a wobbly smile. 'I was a disaster.'

'You weren't bad for a beginner. If it wasn't for your knee, I'd insist you got right back on the ice. But, as it is, you need to rest that knee,' he said.

'I need to sit down; you don't,' she said. 'You're a marvellous skater and you must be itching to do more than you did shepherding me around the rink. Go back and skate.'

He didn't argue and once he had settled her in an observation seat he glided back onto the ice.

There were a lot of people on the rink—some demonstrating incredible skill. But Ashleigh only had eyes for Lukas. In black jeans and a black roll-neck sweater that showed off his athletic physique, he skated fast and skilfully around the perimeter of the rink. As he zoomed past her he raised his hand in a wave and grinned. She waved back, stopped herself from blowing him a kiss. *A friend wouldn't do that.* Somehow he looked younger, more relaxed, happier even. More a regular thirty-four-year-old guy enjoying a physical challenge. The kind of guy she really would like as a friend.

Who was she kidding? She wanted him—more than she had ever wanted a man. In reality, she couldn't be just friends with Lukas. She fancied him too much for there ever to be the comfortable, easy friendship she had with men for whom she felt no attraction. She hadn't lost that urge to push him up against a wall and kiss him—she'd just got better at denying it.

She thrust her hands deep into the pockets of her coat—the lavender one. Thank heaven she hadn't torn or stained it in her fall. Lukas had forbidden her to leave the house in the anorak, which she'd thought was more suitable for ice-skating. Eyes riveted to the rink, she watched him glide and spin and gasped her admiration when he jumped and landed perfectly on the ice.

He was magnificent. She wanted all that energy, all that vigour and passion directed to her. Her body ached for him so much a shiver of pure desire rippled through her. But her heart clamoured for airtime too. This wasn't just about physical attraction—an awareness that had been there from the moment she'd first met him shouting at her to get out of his bathtub. This was so much more.

She was falling in love with him. Against all reason, against all common sense she was falling for him. A lone wolf who had told her he was married to his work. A man who was prepared to manipulate and lie—and coerce her to lie—to get what he wanted. Who was so good at dissembling she didn't know what was real or play-acting.

Ashleigh drew in a breath of the chilly air in an effort to calm the tumult of her emotions. She had to fight this with all her being or she could end up as wounded as she had with Travis, her university heartbreaker, all those years ago. Then she'd been too naive to recognise Travis for what he was. Now Lukas had made it very clear he wasn't the kind for a happy-ever-after. And she wasn't the kind for a meaningless fling. Heck, Lukas hadn't given any indication he was interested enough even for a fling. He had stuck to the letter of their agreement. That passion she'd sensed on the dance floor, coiled ready to be unleashed, had obviously been a figment of her imagination. He was every bit as good an actor as Travis had been.

Lukas skated around the rink more slowly then glided to a halt with an impressive spray of ice. By the time he'd taken off his skates and joined her where she was sitting, she was shivering. He noticed straight away and went to take off his down jacket to put over her shoulders.

'I'm not that cold,' she protested. 'Please keep your coat. Really.'

'Delayed shock from your fall,' he said. 'A hot drink might help.'

She needed a lot more than a hot drink to cure what was ailing her—a kiss would work as a starter—but that was all he had to offer. She would grab what she could in the time she had left with him. *Just friends*, she reminded herself.

Lukas sat opposite Ashleigh in the café that over-looked the rink. He watched the colour return to her cheeks as she sipped on rich, sweet hot chocolate then nibbled on a *churro* dusted with cinnamon and powdered sugar. It left a smear of sugar on her lower lip. He wanted to reach over and wipe it away with his finger. Better, to press his mouth against hers and lick it, to test which tasted sweeter—the sugar or her delicious mouth.

'Feeling better?' he asked.

She nodded. 'Although my pride might take a while to recover from its battering.'

She took another sip of her chocolate. To his

intense disappointment it washed away the smear of sugar.

'May I suggest you get some tuition from a professional next time you hit the ice?' he said. 'A lesson or two to get you started and, with your dancing skills, you'll soon be spinning with the best of them.'

'Thank you for that vote of confidence,' she said. She didn't like to fail, he realised. 'You were awesome on the ice.'

'I learned as a kid. I guess you didn't get much opportunity to ice-skate in your home town.' Curious about her background, he'd looked up Bundaberg on the Internet.

'You're right there,' she said. 'There are indoor ice rinks in Brisbane, where I went to university, but I wasn't really interested. It's here that's the attraction. London. Even though I was a dud on skates, the experience of being here counts for everything.'

'Yet surely you must miss being home for Christmas. From what you say, you're very close to your family.'

That closeness and sense of belonging was something he found himself envying. Christmas seemed to magnify the sterility of his own family life. Not that he should care. That little rich boy who had to fly to a council house in Birmingham to experience a loving family Christmas had long grown up into a man who had given up hope that the festive season would ever mean anything to him again.

'Of course I do,' she said. 'This will be the first Christmas I've spent apart from my family. It will feel weird not to be with them.'

'Why not fly home for a few days and come back to London?'

She rubbed her thumb against her first two fingers together to signify lack of cash. He could pay for her fare if she really wanted to go. 'But it isn't just the money. It's…complicated.'

'How do you mean?'

She paused and he could tell by the expressions that flickered across her face she was debating whether or not to tell him. 'Because my family are insisting on inviting my ex for Christmas and I don't want to be there if he's there.'

He frowned. 'Your family would choose your former fiancé over you?'

'So it seems,' she said, her lush mouth trembling with hurt and betrayal.

'Why would they do such a thing?'

'In some misguided attempt at getting us to reconcile, I suspect,' she said, compressing her lips to a tight line.

'They must believe that there's a case for that.'

Her pale redhead's skin flushed. 'Please don't tell me you're another one who doesn't believe a twenty-seven-year-old woman who decided she didn't want to marry a guy would have cancelled a wedding and burdened herself with debt if she didn't really mean it.'

'So tell me why your family thinks this way. It puzzles me.' He remembered how convincing Céline had been that everything had been over with her boyfriend back home.

Ashleigh rested on her elbows and leaned across the table towards him. 'Let me tell you about Dan. His mother was friends with my mother. The mums were delighted when they had babies within six months of each other—Dan being born first. We were destined to be together, according to them. Actually, we were thrown together so much we did become childhood friends. Dan was the closest thing I had to a brother. But he was always teasing me and it bugged me. As we got into our teens it got worse; he was trying to get my attention I see now. I avoided him. The joke that we'd get married when we grew up wore very thin. Then we went away to Manchester. When I got back for my final year of high school Dan had grown up into the handsomest boy in the school.'

'And you fell for him.'

'He was hot. I was flattered he still only had eyes for me. We dated. But we were kids. I didn't want just the one boyfriend.'

'High school is much too young to be serious,' he said. Yet some of his friends had married their teenage sweethearts and were happy. In fact, they felt sorry for him, single at thirty-four. He was only alone because he wanted to be, he reminded himself. Or because he had never met a woman who made him think otherwise. Until now. Until *this* woman, who was still entangled with another man.

'I broke it off with him when I went to university,' she said, continuing her story. 'I wanted to explore new interests, new friendships.'

'How did he take it?' It was difficult for him to hear this, to think of her with that other man. He forced himself to act the disinterested friend.

She shrugged. 'Okay, I thought. But it didn't seem to change things with him. "I'm always here for you," he'd say.'

'To cut a long story short, I had my heart badly broken at uni, then made a few rotten choices that also ended badly. But when I went home to Bundaberg on vacation, there was always Dan waiting there with a shoulder to cry on and to bolster my ego. I began to think I couldn't do better than Dan. He wouldn't hurt me. We started dating again. Our families were delighted. I... I chose the safe harbour rather than the wild, tumultuous waves that had thrown me so painfully on the rocks when they'd finished with me.'

'Were you happy with him?' He hated the thought of her with another man yet he had to ask.

Her mouth twisted. 'If happy meant the absence of pain and angst. If happy meant comfortable and predictable. If happy meant being bored but telling myself that was the price for security.'

'And Dan?' The man had kept taking her

back—and Lukas would bet he would do it again. It wouldn't surprise him to find the Australian on his doorstep in Chelsea wanting to know where his bride was. Then he, Lukas, would be pushed aside.

'Here's the weird thing—he was the son of my mother's best friend. When his parents split up it was like he moved onto family number two. It became like he wanted to marry into my family as much as he wanted me. The more certain of me he got, the more he bonded with my parents and sister. The teasing started again. I began to feel undermined, disrespected, ganged up on. They'd laugh off my protests as if I was a kid. In the end I'd had enough. You know the rest.'

'Yet your family seem convinced you'll go back to him. Again.'

'Aaargh!' She mimed tearing out her lovely red hair. 'Even you don't believe me. I will *never* go back to Dan. *Ever.* I started to drown in that safe harbour. And now... Well, now I want the wild sea. I want the passion. And I want a man who'll ride those waves with me and only *me*.'

Her eyes sparked that blue fire that excited him. She held his gaze. Was there a message there for him? Or was he seeing what he wanted to see? Eventually, she dropped her eyes. He remembered just days ago she'd sworn she wanted to stay single. Now she wanted a man to give her passion. Why had she changed her mind? Because of *him*? A tiny flame of hope flickered to life in his heart that had been so cold for so long.

'So now you know why I will not be going back to Bundaberg for Christmas,' she said emphatically.

Lukas still wasn't sure he believed her. She drained her hot chocolate. Picked up the remaining crumbs of her *churro* with her finger and licked them off with the tip of her pink, pointy tongue accompanied by a throaty little murmur of appreciation. Was she doing this to provoke him? Or did she just like *churros*?

'What about you, Lukas? When do you fly to Athens?'

'I don't,' he said. 'I'm staying here in London.'

Her eyes widened. 'But you said you always spend Christmas in Athens.'

'This year is the exception. Rather than endure another of my parents' idea of a festive celebration, I decided to spend Christmas Day on my own in one of my favourite houses in one of my favourite cities.'

'Oh,' she said. 'I was planning to travel to Manchester to spend the day with Sophie and her family but if you're here on your own I'll—'

'Please don't change your plans on my account. I'm happy to be here on my own. I *want* to be here on my own.' But, once planted, the thought did not go away. Christmas Day with just Ashleigh and him in the house...

'I don't like the thought of you being in London all by yourself,' she said. But he only saw friendly concern in her eyes. He could not read more into it—that would only lead to disillusion and the kind of pain he had protected himself against for so long.

He glanced down at his watch. 'I enjoyed today. Thank you for getting me away from my computer. It did me good.'

She smiled. 'I'm glad. You see, I'm on a mission for you to stop being such a workaholic and enjoy life. As I said earlier, what's the point of being a billionaire if you don't have fun?'

'Work is fun—maybe you have yet to learn that,' he said.

She was right, but he wasn't going to admit it. He was too used to guarding himself, to not admitting to anything that could be perceived as weakness. A kind of myth had developed around him in his country—the invincible young man who had modernised a product, turned around a company, transformed loss into soaring profit and created sorely needed jobs at a time of economic disaster. If the distribution deal with Tina worked out, and his marketing people did their work—which they would or they would lose those jobs—a new market meant more opportunities for his company and his people.

'Perhaps,' she said. 'In the new year I'll have to seriously think about what I'm doing here. Waitressing is all very well in the short term but it's not a career.' She dimpled at him. 'Nor is being your maid.' He wanted her as so much more than a maid. But the thought that she intended to stay in London further fanned the new hope in his heart.

'Will you look for work as an accountant?'

'Probably. You know Tina offered to help me?'

'No. You didn't tell me that.' He felt uncomfortable at the thought that Ashleigh might step out of line. Dealing with Tina Norris was not her place. And he didn't trust Tina's motives.

'Don't look so annoyed,' she said. 'Of course I thanked her but obviously it will never happen. I won't ever see her again.'

'No,' he said. And very soon he'd be saying goodbye to Ashleigh.

It was not a happy thought.

CHAPTER TWELVE

ASHLEIGH SPENT A delightful day on Sunday with Emma and the other two bridesmaids, Sophie and Grace. She also met Emma's childhood friend and sister-in-law, Clare, who was to be Emma's chief bridesmaid. Ashleigh liked Clare immediately. She felt she was building real friends—important if she were to stay indefinitely in the UK. Bundaberg seemed a long way away, a different world. *And too far away from Lukas,* an insistent voice from deep in her heart reminded her.

They enjoyed the morning at Sophie's tiny flat in the furthermost edge of Chelsea, trying on their bridesmaid outfits, exquisite vintage-style dresses in a dusky pink silk trimmed with antique lace. When the others marvelled at how quickly she'd got the dresses to fitting stage, Sophie explained she'd already had the fabric, purchased ages ago at a market.

The four bridesmaids braved the Christmas

crowds to shop for shoes in Oxford Street and had a delightfully girly lunch in the stylish café in Selfridges department store. Ashleigh couldn't help contrasting Emma's confidence and joy in making plans for her renewed marriage to how she'd felt planning her wedding to Dan.

She'd been irritable, snappy, picking fault with the dresses, the caterer's menu, with everything. Deep down she'd known marrying him wasn't right. She should have listened to her instinct earlier. That same instinct that was telling her that if she ever had a chance to be with Lukas it would be earth-shatteringly wonderful—wild waves the like of which she had never imagined existed. If only she had even an inkling that he might feel the same.

But when her friends asked her how things were going with the 'pretend boyfriend' she just described the Butterfly Ball and the show dance and told them how well the outfit they'd helped her buy had been received. Her feelings for Lukas were something to be hugged to herself.

After she said goodbye to her friends she went back to Chelsea via Harrods, where she bought decorations for Lukas's house—exquisite glass baubles and ornaments and a beautifully crafted artificial tree.

He wasn't at the house so she put them up alone, giving in to the indulgence of imagining how very different it would be if they were decorating his house together. Lukas and her getting into the spirit of Christmas, Lukas reaching up to help her put the star at the top of the tree, Lukas manoeuvring her under the mistletoe she'd hung in the hallway.

Her sigh echoed through the empty living room. *Wasn't going to happen.* But at least he would celebrate his solitary Christmas Day with some of the festive trimmings in his fabulous house. Maybe, just maybe, they might inspire thoughts of her.

The next morning, Ashleigh lay in Lukas's guest bed for longer than she should have. She counted down the remaining days until she'd have to kiss its featherbed luxury goodbye and head for the dubious comfort of Sophie's sofa with the broken spring. The plan was she would pack her bag on Christmas Eve, head up to Manchester with Sophie and then return to her London flat with Sophie the day after Boxing Day. All her borrowed finery would stay behind in this room. With one exception. There was just one thing she was determined to take with her—too bad the possible consequences.

Her smartphone buzzed the presence of an incoming text message. If it was Dan or her parents or her sister begging her to reconsider her decision to come home for Christmas she'd throw the phone at the wall. But it was from Lukas, asking her to meet him in his study at her earliest opportunity. Her heart sank right to the level of the basement kitchen. So this was it. Eviction time.

She got dressed with hands that shook so much she could barely pull up the zip on her jeans and drag a long-sleeved black T-shirt over her head.

Then she was in his office, back where they'd started—him handsome and imposing on one side of the desk, her the intruder on the other.

But he got up to greet her with the biggest smile she'd seen on his face. Her heart seemed to flip inside her at how handsome he looked, his dark eyes lit with excitement. 'Good news. Tina has signed our agreement. We'll be doing business.'

'That's great news,' she said, forcing enthusiasm into her voice. 'Congratulations.'

'Our strategy paid off,' he said.

Now he had no need for her—she was meant to be delighted about that? 'So it's over. The pretend boyfriend and girlfriend thing, I mean,' she said dully. In truth, she was glad about that part. Keeping up the charade had become too difficult. Not when she wanted it to be something unscripted and genuine.

'Not quite,' he said. 'Tina has invited us to celebrate with her tonight at her Mayfair apartment for drinks.' How casually he included her as the other half of the *us* equation.

Panic threatened to choke her reply. She couldn't do this. Not now. She could no longer pretend feelings for him that had become so painfully real. Her gaze darted around the room, to his rows of books in both English and Greek, the blue paperweight on his desk that was a Greek charm against the evil eye—intrigued, she'd looked it up when she'd first dusted his desk—anywhere but at him. 'I… I can't… I just—'

'Just one more time, Ashleigh. Please.' Finally, she faced him to see an expression she hadn't seen before on his features. A subtle shift. Not pleading. Not demanding. Just asking a favour of an equal. 'Because we're friends now,' he said.

How could she refuse when he played that card? She nodded, still having difficulty with her words.

'Thank you,' he said, with a sincerity that was new to her. 'This deal is important. Not just to me and my company. But to my country, which needs the employment and the tax revenue it will bring. These are troubling times.'

Again she nodded. There was so much more to this man than she had imagined on that first meeting in this room when he had threatened her with jail. She ached to know him better. Would she ever get the chance?

'This will mean more shopping, I'm afraid,' he said.

She managed a wobbly smile. 'You're afraid?' she said. 'When you've just uttered words that are magic to a woman's ears?'

He smiled back and for a long moment her eyes locked with his. Surely there was something new there. Amusement? Affection? Whatever it was, it warmed her. *Even if it was only friendship.*

She would love to be able to hand him back his credit card and tell him she would buy her own new clothes for the drinks with Tina. But she needed every penny for when she had to find accommodation in the new year. And he wanted her to look the part of his consort. She looked down at her jeans. 'So I guess I'd better get into my shopping outfit,' she said.

'You'll enjoy it more if you do,' he said.

She held her breath, hoping he would say he would accompany her. When he didn't, she let it out on a sigh that was disappointment edged with relief. Maybe it was for the best. Having him there with her, assessing her choices through narrowed, sexy eyes would only make her life more difficult than it had suddenly become. *In love with her billionaire boss.* How could she have been so foolish to let this happen?

'A dress, do you think?' she asked.

'You've done everything right so far,' he said. 'I'll leave it to you.'

Now that her use to him was nearly at an end he didn't care. She forced a smile on her face as she thanked him.

* * *

Of course Ashleigh had got it right, Lukas thought that evening as Tina welcomed them to her apartment. As she'd done from the get-go. Poised and elegant, Ashleigh wore a fitted black dress with strategically placed sheer panels that sent a man's imagination into a frenzy but didn't actually reveal anything. She'd bought new shoes too—sexy black stilettos with a flat bow on the front and laced around her ankles. With his mother's coat flung over the top, she looked perfect for the part she was about to play for the last time.

'Welcome,' Tina effused. 'I'm so glad you two were available to toast the sealing of our deal.' As if he'd had a choice—this deal was too important to risk offending her.

Tina air-kissed Lukas on each cheek then did the same to Ashleigh. 'I'm so glad we'll be doing business together,' Tina said.

But Lukas wasn't sure if she was directing her words to him or to Ashleigh. Both of them, he supposed, as Tina made such a big deal of vetting people's spouses. He didn't trust the way the older woman had suggested she could help Ashleigh find a job. That was not part of the remit. It could be ulterior motive on her part, but then again she seemed to genuinely like Ashleigh.

Tina might even be disappointed when, after a decent interval, he informed her that Ashleigh had decided he was merely a rebound guy and had moved on. A cold sweat broke out on his forehead. Forget Tina. *He* would be gutted when she was no longer around.

A pleasant-looking young man offered them champagne flutes from a silver tray. Lukas grabbed one. *He needed a drink.* Lukas took the guy for a waiter. He was shocked when the waiter took a glass for himself. Even more shocked when Tina smiled and introduced him as her boyfriend, Gary.

Lukas caught Ashleigh's eye. She discreetly raised her eyebrows, obviously as surprised as he was. Lukas's first reaction was relief. So the cougar had found herself a toy boy. That took him completely off the hook. He still shuddered at the memory of that older woman friend of his mother's invading his bedroom.

But then, when both couples were seated together on the cream sofas in Tina's small but elegantly appointed living room, he noticed the

body language between Tina and Gary and wondered what was really going on. There was something genuine there. Not something to make fun
of.

'Your apartment is beautiful,' said Ashleigh to
kick off the conversation.

'Couldn't afford it now,' said Tina with typical
bluntness. 'My father bought it as a pied-à-terre
back in the nineteen sixties. These days Mayfair
is a cosmopolitan outpost of Moscow and Dubai
and prices are astronomical.'

'Indeed,' said Lukas. He didn't like to discuss
his personal finances with anyone other than his
bankers. In fact he felt uncomfortable discussing
anything personal with anyone.

Gary squeezed Tina's hand and got up from the
sofa. 'I'm sure you'd like some food,' he said. He
shared Tina's Liverpudlian accent.

'Gary is a chef,' Tina explained as her eyes
followed the younger man from the room. 'He
works for the catering company I use in Liverpool. But he's cooked for us tonight as my man.'
She seemed to take extraordinary pleasure from
the words *my man*.

'He seems very nice,' said Ashleigh diplomatically.

'That he is,' said Tina. 'I've known him a while. Always liked him. He liked me. But he's twenty-five and I'm forty-five. It seemed impossible.'

'No one would blink an eyelid if your ages were reversed,' Ashleigh said. 'Why should it matter? Besides, you don't look older at all.' *Well done, Ashleigh*, Lukas thought. Though she was only stretching the truth a little. No way did Tina look forty-five.

'I began to realise that,' Tina said. 'But it was you who finally made me see it.'

'Me?' said Ashleigh.

'Ashleigh?' said Lukas at the same time.

Tina addressed Ashleigh. 'The night we met for dinner when you said love comes when you're not looking for it. When that person comes along who makes you feel only half alive when you're apart. That's how I felt about Gary. And, happily, how he felt about me. I didn't invite him to the Butterfly Ball, too worried what people might think. I missed him so much all night. Seeing you two so happy, so in love, made me realise there was no running from what I felt any more.'

We're not in love. Lukas had to stop the words from blurting out. He noticed Ashleigh frown. Because she didn't like the idea of him being in love with her? Or because he didn't acknowledge Tina's words?

'That's such a lovely story, Tina,' said Ashleigh with a warm, genuine smile. 'I'm glad I was of some help, even inadvertently.' Not only was Ashleigh beautiful, she was kind and warm and supportive—everything he'd thought he would never find in a woman.

One thing was for certain—he intended to politely eat some of Gary's superb hors d'oeuvres and then get the hell away from this place. He had to be alone with Ashleigh. Once and for all, he had to see if there was something real between them.

It was as if all Ashleigh's fantasies had come to life. As soon as she and Lukas reached the pavement outside Tina's apartment, he turned her to him, looked deep into her face. She thrilled to the intensity of his eyes, the way they narrowed as he searched her face, the sensual half curve of his mouth. Then, without a word, he pulled her close to him.

Finally, the truth—no words required. His quickened breathing told her all she needed to know. *He wanted her as much as she wanted him.* Her gasp of impatience, of *want*, no doubt sent the same message to him.

Then his mouth was on hers, hard, warm, exciting, demanding a response. She parted her lips, welcomed him, kissed him back. It felt as if she'd waited all her life for this. For *him*. It hadn't started sweet and gentle and went straight to deep and demanding—an urgent meeting of mouths and tongues, of bodies straining hard against each other. His overcoat was open. She splayed her hands on his hard chest and pushed him to the wall behind him. *At last.* This. *Lukas.* Her heart thudded loud and fast. He slid his hands inside her coat, to pull her close—as close as she could be to his body through layers of winter clothes. Her nipples tightened as desire pulsed through her in a wave that demanded more. He held her so close to his body she felt his response, hard and insistent, which further inflamed her. *She wanted him.*

'Lukas,' she moaned. 'Why did we wait so long for this?'

He stilled. She knew immediately she'd said the wrong thing. 'We didn't,' he said, his voice hoarse and strained. 'I've only known you a week.'

'That's long enough,' she said, her voice raspy with desire.

'For what?'

'For this,' she said, lifting her face to his, hungry for his mouth to possess hers again.

'For a one-night stand?' He broke away from her. 'Because that's all I can give you.'

'Not even a two-night stand?' she asked, trying to lighten the tension, succeeding in making it worse.

He made his *humph* sound but it didn't sound in the slightest bit amusing.

'I scarcely know you but you're making me feel things I don't want to feel, feelings I've lived without for a long time,' he said roughly. Was that an edge of panic to his voice? 'I can't give you what you want.'

She could feel a red flush rising on her neck. 'How do you know what I want? How do you know I don't just want to drag you into the back seat of the car and make crazy, heart-pounding, toe-tingling love with you—then walk away from you when it's over?'

'Because you'll want more.'

'I might. The way I feel about you, once wouldn't be enough. I mean, if it was really toe-tingling...' Her voice trailed away at his desolate expression.

'I meant more than I can give. Commitment. Marriage. Presumably children.'

Ashleigh stared at him in disbelief. 'I'm sick of people telling me what I want. You included. How can you possibly presume to know what drives me? I want you— I want you desperately. I won't lie about that.'

'I want you too,' he muttered.

'But not enough to believe it might be worth taking a risk on me? That there might be *more*? You're from a different world but I don't think this kind of...of *feeling* comes along very often whether you live in Athens or in London or in Bundaberg. Maybe...maybe only once in a life-time.'

She turned her face from him, not wanting him to read the depth of her despair that this might be all she would ever have of him. Knowing she could not even hint at *love*. 'Or maybe we've made such a good job of pretence it seems real, when…when in reality there's nothing there.'

A group of people turned the corner into Tina's street and headed towards them. Mayfair was full of clubs and restaurants. It was a miracle there'd been no one around to witness their exchange. She stood in silence looking up at Lukas, until the group staggered by with generalised greetings of 'Merry Christmas' fading away with them.

'Merry Christmas,' she responded in a low choked voice she wondered if the revellers even heard.

Lukas's face was set like granite, his mouth a grim, hard line. 'All my life I haven't known who was genuine or what their motives were.'

'Well, please don't dump me in the same basket as people who…who might have injured you.' Ashleigh cursed her redhead's temper after the words slipped out—she hadn't meant to be hurtful.

She wiped her hand over her forehead. Wrapped her borrowed coat tight across her. Forced away the memory of how exciting his hands had felt on her body through the fine fabric of her dress. How much more she wanted than those brief, passionate moments. 'I'm sorry. I… I think I had too much champagne and not enough of Gary's snacks.'

In truth she'd been too eager to get away from Tina and Gary and to be alone with Lukas to bother with eating. Only to be lifted up on a wild wave of desire and exultation that he wanted her, then to crash painfully back down on the rocks to whimper and nurse her wounds. But she wasn't the whimpering type. She would not give in to the tears of disappointment that burned behind her eyes. Instead she tossed her head and strode as fast as she could on her stilettos away from him.

The car was a few houses away, the driver sitting patiently waiting for them. She headed towards it, was aware of Lukas close behind.

Why did she get the feeling that it was going to be another journey back to Chelsea—she could never think of the townhouse as *home*—with her and Lukas sitting in grim silence? Especially when thoughts of what she'd told him she'd like to do with him in that very back seat would not be easy to suppress.

Ashleigh checked her watch in the dark. Three a.m. She'd gone straight to her room when they'd got home, wanting to avoid Lukas at all cost. Now she was hungry.

She used the light from her phone to guide her down the stairs to the kitchen. The elevator might be too noisy and alert Lukas to her presence. If he was still in the house, that was. He could easily have gone out and she wouldn't have heard him.

He hadn't left the house. As she pushed open the door of the basement kitchen she saw him sitting in the same chair where he'd been last time, in a dim pool of light from the pendant lights that hung over the table. He had his head resting on his arms on the table. The back of his neck looked somehow vulnerable—not something she had ever expected to think about Lukas Christophedes. A great rush of tenderness for him swept over her. *Oh, she had it bad.*

'Lukas,' she said softly. 'Are you awake?'

He nodded.

This time she didn't resist the urge to go to him,

this the last night she would spend in his house, maybe the last time she would ever see him. She stood behind him, leaned down, circled her arms around him and placed her cheek against his. His stubble was deliciously scratchy against her skin. She breathed in his already so familiar scent. Felt the wave of want for him that she doubted would ever go away. Silently, he reached up to put his hand on her arm.

'You okay?' she asked, emboldened because she couldn't sink any lower than she already had with her suggestion of having her way with him in the back seat of his car.

'I felt hungry,' he said. 'But I got down here and it all seemed too much effort.'

'I guess you're used to having staff,' she said. Staff like *her*.

'I actually don't need staff to toast a piece of bread,' he said gruffly.

She released him from her arms and stood up straight. 'The staff is on board now. Let me make you some toast. There's pizza in the freezer if you want me to—'

He got up, blocked her with his body from heading to the freezer. 'You're not staff.'

She looked up at him. His eyes were blood-shot and weary. 'I actually am. You pay Maids in Chelsea for me to be your full-time maid.'

'You are *not* my maid. Not any more.' He didn't touch her, just looked down into her face.

'Then what am I, Lukas? Not your pretend girl-friend—the need for that is over; you've done your deal. Not your friend either. I want you too much to keep up the pretence of being a platonic friend. Not even your lover—despite the…the de-sire we so obviously feel for each other.'

He swore under his breath in Greek. She didn't understand a word of it, which was probably just as well. 'I don't know who you are to me,' he said finally. 'I don't know who the real Ashleigh is. You are such a good actress. You fooled Tina, you confused me. Sometimes I think you could transform my life; other times I'm not certain I know you at all.'

'I have been no one but myself,' she said. 'What you've seen are different facets of me. I was never dishonest with you. Ever. Except when I hid my attraction for you, not dreaming you felt any-thing for me. But tonight…well, tonight I bared my heart to you. Yet you can't seem to trust me.'

He acknowledged that with a slow nod. 'I have an issue with trust—especially with women.' Would he ever share what had put those shadows behind his eyes?

'I've got every reason not to trust you either,' she said. 'You're not bad at pretending to be someone you're not. You made our fake date scenarios as real as I did. But I liked everything I saw about you. I *like* you, Lukas, as well as being crazy attracted to you.'

'How do I know what is real about you and what is façade?' he asked. 'I thought my mother was a devoted wife. Until I walked in on her with another man at one of the decadent parties my parents were famed for in Athens. I discovered both my parents had multiple affairs. My father from the beginning of the marriage. My mother in retaliation when she found out about his. I grew up shielding my mother from my father's lies—and vice versa. I knew more than a child should know about my parents' private lives. I learned to hide my feelings. They only stayed together for my sake, so they told me. Though why they are still together now, I don't know.'

'I'm sorry,' she murmured. Not in a million

years could she imagine her parents holding dec-adent parties and finding lovers. In spite of the gravity of it, she smiled to herself. There'd be no holding onto those kinds of secrets in a country town.

She brushed past him, thrilling in the contact no matter how brief. Put a saucepan of milk on the stove to boil. Hot chocolate might be required if she was ever to sleep again tonight. She put thick slices of wholewheat bread in the toaster.

'That must have been difficult for a kid to cope with.'

'The worst was to come,' said Lukas with a grimace. 'A few days before I turned twenty-one I discovered they had totally mismanaged the company that my grandfather had spent his life building up. It was on the verge of bankruptcy and yet they still kept on spending, milking the company to fund their lavish lifestyle.'

'And it was up to you to save it. Still a boy. What had you intended to do instead?'

'All my life I had wanted to be an architect. Growing up in a city where everywhere there are reminders of our great civilisation, I was in-spired to make my own mark on the landscape.'

'But you had to give up your studies?'

'Yes. And my dreams.' Disappointment and regret threaded through his words.

'From what you've told me, you've made your mark in a different way. You must be proud of what you accomplished.'

'My family were very grateful. They got to keep everything. They didn't care that I had to remove them as directors.'

'That must have been difficult.'

'You can't imagine what it was like to unravel the mess they'd made—the lies, the deception, the payments to mistresses, even blackmail.'

'No wonder you have an issue with trust,' she said. 'But now, as an adult, having gone through all that, surely you feel able to make your own judgement of who is genuine and who is not?' *Surely you could believe in me?*

He shrugged. 'Perhaps my judgement was distorted.' He told her about a girl named Céline who had deceived him and broken his heart. 'I believed in her yet she turned out to be not the person I thought she was. Like my mother. Like my father.'

'We've all had our hearts broken,' Ashleigh

said. 'But we have to learn from it. Not that I'm any great example; look how long I took to do the right thing with Dan. The right thing for him too, I now realise. He's actually not a bad guy and deserves someone who genuinely loves him. I wasted his time as well as mine because I was scared of getting dumped by the waves.'

'How do I do that?' He seemed genuinely puzzled.

'You have to listen to your instinct; you have to *feel* what is right rather than try to intellectualise it or, worse, block it with fear.'

'Like when you're dancing,' he said slowly.

'Exactly. The steps are nothing without the emotion. You have to feel the dance.'

He frowned. 'How do you trust your feelings when they are so abstract?'

'Is that a trick question?' She took the milk off the stovetop. 'Why is a successful billionaire asking me that?'

He shook his head. 'I genuinely want to know.'

'Surely you trust your instinct when it comes to business? You couldn't have got to where you are without doing that.'

'Success involves facts and figures and market analysis and—'

'Knowing when to take a risk or make a gamble?'

'That too,' he said. 'I can trust a gamble informed by research. I will never be able to make life-changing decisions based on something as ephemeral as *feeling*.'

'You're serious about that?'

'Of course. What other answer could I give?'

The toast popped out of the toaster. 'Peanut butter?' she asked. The pantry was packed with jars of an American brand so she assumed it was his favourite.

She spread both pieces of toast thickly, cut them in half, put them on a plate and slid it across the table to him.

'Aren't you having any?' he asked.

'I'm not hungry any more,' she said. 'A milky drink will do me fine.'

The illusion of intimacy in the semi-darkened kitchen was seductive. But she could not stay here. She was beginning to believe he was right. *He could not give her what she needed.* He would destroy her if she kept on throwing herself against an emotional brick wall. *Maybe he didn't know how to love.*

She waited for him to finish his toast. Her drink stayed untouched in the mug.

She took the plate and the mug to the sink and rinsed them like a good maid should. Delaying. Wanting these last moments alone with him. Until the tension made her feel nauseous.

'Lukas, I've packed. I'm leaving in the morning.'

Was that relief that flashed across his face? Not regret or hurt or anger? She felt as if he had plunged a knife into her heart.

'You don't have to do that,' he said. It *was* relief. Her stomach roiled.

'I promised you could stay until after—'

'Christmas. I know. But you have no further use for me. And I… I have to get on with my life.' *Beg me to stay, Lukas, beg me to stay.*

But he didn't.

'Where will you go?' he asked. The knife twisted deeper.

'The renewal of vows ceremony is on Wednesday at The Daphne Hotel in Cadogan Gardens. My friend has booked rooms for her bridesmaids for Tuesday and Wednesday nights. Thursday is

Christmas Eve and I'll go to Manchester with Sophie.'

Silence hung between them for a long, uncomfortable moment.

'If you decide you want to go back to Australia for Christmas, I'll buy you a ticket.'

She stared at him. '*What?* Why would I want to do that?'

The expression on his face told her everything.

'After all I've told you—you still think I want to go back to Dan? You still don't trust me? Yet I have more cause not to trust *you* and I was prepared to take the risk. You just don't get it, do you, Lukas?'

She took his hand and placed it on her chest where her heart was furiously pounding. 'Do you feel that, Lukas? Do you? That's my heart pounding for *you*. Not Dan. Not any other man. But *you*.'

She kept his hand over her heart for a long moment. *Can't you feel it breaking, Lukas?* Then dropped his hand and turned on her heel.

Ashleigh lay on her back on her bed until the light filtered through the curtains. Then picked up her backpack and the one Bond Street shopping bag she'd vowed to save and left it all behind her. The clothes, the shoes, the watch. *Lukas.* They had never belonged to her.

The only thing she would take with her that she hadn't come with was Lukas's scarf he had loaned her that first night. Her breath hitched as she buried her face in its soft warmth and breathed in his scent before she wrapped the scarf around her neck and tucked the ends over her heart.

CHAPTER THIRTEEN

YOU JUST WANT to be with that one special person. You feel only half alive when you're apart.

Ashleigh's words echoed through Lukas and made the weight in his chest feel even heavier. Now he knew exactly what she'd meant. *Too late* he knew what she'd meant.

She had been gone a day. And it was as if a light had been switched off—not just in his house but in his soul. How could one woman make such an impact on his life in such a short time? She had urged him to *feel* it—to feel her heartbeat as if it might somehow kick-start his own. But there was a void there. Why was it that some part of him that processed emotions seemed so shut off and inaccessible?

Until Ashleigh had breezed into his life on a cloud of bubbles and opened just a crack that was slowly, painfully being pushed apart.

He sat at his desk and tried to work—his great

solace, his great distraction. Had he actually told her that work was *fun*? But the more he tried to focus on the overall strategy for his move into the UK market, the more thoughts of Ashleigh kept slamming into his mind and knocking his concentration sidewards.

Fun was stumbling on the ice with Ashleigh. *Fun* was feeling the rhythm of the dance with her. *Fun* was holding in his arms the loveliest woman he had ever met—lovely in both face and spirit.

She spoke of trust. He realised he had an abiding distrust of women. His mother, the first betrayal. Then his nanny, falling in love and marrying a Greek boy from a town too far away for the young Lukas to visit. She hadn't abandoned him completely. He was still in touch with her, even now. But he had loved her more than anyone and had not been allowed to express it for fear of offending his mother. Then he had allowed Céline to shatter his trust—foolishly now, he saw. He should have treated that as the fling it so obviously had been for her. But Ashleigh had not lied to him—he had asked her to lie *for* him.

Nevertheless, the fear was there. If he made himself vulnerable to her—the first woman since Céline to make him want to—he could end up wounded beyond endurance. With all the responsibility for his family on his shoulders—the son holding up the parents instead of the usual way of things—he could not afford the distraction. Yet if he did not—what kind of empty life stretched out ahead of him?

By his persistence in thinking she would betray him and return to her former fiancé, had he driven Ashleigh away? Had he ever really heard her?

The house was very quiet. Too quiet. He usually took delight in solitude. But he longed to hear the most tuneless version of *Jingle Bells* ever sung coming from his bathroom. Instead there was nothing. The ticking of the grandfather clock in the hallway below had always sounded comforting. Now it sounded ominous. Each second taking her further away from him.

He gave up on work. Found himself heading in the direction of her bedroom. He pushed open the door—almost expecting her to be there. A remnant of her scent danced in the air—fresh and sweet. Lukas closed his eyes the better to inhale it.

When he opened them, he was shocked to see she'd left everything he'd bought her behind, neatly packed in the closet. It was bitterly cold today; snow was predicted for Christmas Day. He was angry at her for not taking at least the coat and the boots. She would be freezing in that old anorak.

But she had left something else behind. A small gift-wrapped box on the dressing table. He picked it up, was stunned to see it was for him. He read the tasteful Christmas tag.

To Lukas—good luck.
A xx

With hands that weren't steady he tore open the wrapping. It was a hand-blown glass ornament in the shape of a pomegranate, its rich colour picked out with gold. Lukas remembered telling her about the Greek tradition where a pomegranate was hung above the front door for Christmas. He was touched by her thoughtfulness. Of the many lavish gifts he had been given over the years, this was the most precious by far.

Lukas turned the card over.

P.S. This was not *paid for with your credit card.*

He was *feeling* it now all right. Loss. Regret. A deep, aching need for her. And, overriding it all—*hope.*

She did not intend to come back. He'd found her keys and the credit card on the hallway table. He hadn't needed to see them to know she was gone. He had *felt* the emptiness of the house.

But if she felt a fraction of the emotion that was building in him he might be able to convince her to come back. He had to find her. Apologise. Explain. Grovel if he had to. And he had to go armed with something to convince her of the truth about how he felt.

He thought of the many kiss-off pieces of jewellery he had purchased to signal the end with a woman who had started pushing him for more. The only kind of jewellery he wanted to buy for Ashleigh was something she'd wear on the third finger of her left hand and that he'd be around to admire until death did them part.

She'd told him where she was staying. He had

to go find her. He wanted her. And he didn't stop until he got what he wanted.

But then the phone rang.

Ashleigh stood with the other bridesmaids, lined up alongside Emma under the elegant floral arch in the main reception room at The Daphne Hotel. She was enthralled as she witnessed Emma and Jack renew their vows six years after they had married in secret as teenagers. There was something heart-wrenchingly beautiful about celebrating a relationship that was already deeply committed and had been forged through hardship and separation. These two deserved their happiness.

They were the Earl and Countess of Redminster, high up on the social scale that was the English aristocracy. Yet today, here, they were simply a man and a woman in love, celebrating that love with a select few family and friends. Ashleigh felt honoured to be part of the bridal party.

Jack was so tall and protective, Emma slender and golden in the strikingly elegant white dress designed by Sophie, with flowers twisted through her blonde hair. Love and trust and faith shone from their eyes as they made promises to each other. To love. To honour. In sickness and in health.

Could she have felt that for Lukas? The painful lurch in her heart told her *yes*. Or had she fallen for a man who didn't really exist? Real or not, she'd been grateful she'd had the wedding preparations to distract her. Because that man she had only known such a short time had left a big, aching gap in her life. All this happiness, all this talk of love made her feel that loss even more. For the first time since she'd been in London, she felt lonely.

Emma and Jack concluded the ceremony with the sweetest of kisses that made the bridesmaids sigh. Then the couple was immediately surrounded by well-wishers—including Emma's mother and her second husband, who had come from France. Clio Caldwell was there too, in the company of an intriguingly handsome man who could rival Lukas for dark, Mediterranean good looks. Was that an engagement ring flashing on Clio's finger? Standing at a distance, emanating disapproval, were Jack's parents. Apparently, they would never forgive Emma for the scandal that had enveloped her father and dragged her along with it.

Parents, Ashleigh mused. Here they were in their mid- to late twenties—Lukas in his thirties—still being affected by their parents and their behaviour. It sounded as if Lukas's family had been dysfunctional at best; no wonder he'd learned to tamp down on his emotions for self-protection. Except for their inexplicable obsession with Dan, Ashleigh's parents were almost boringly normal and she wouldn't have them any other way.

The thought struck her that perhaps she'd been striving for the kind of marriage her parents had when she'd agreed to marry Dan. Thank heaven she'd run, because now she'd tasted fireworks with Lukas, she knew nothing else would do. *Ever.*

Lukas had no trouble getting past reception at the quirky Chelsea hotel and through to the ballroom where the renewal of vows ceremony was being held for the Earl and Countess of Redminister. Another thing he didn't know about Ashleigh—

he'd had no idea she had connections with the cream of this country's aristocracy. She could hold her own anywhere, as she'd proved again and again. But all he wanted was for her to find her place in his heart.

The ceremony was concluding as he made his way quietly to the back of the room. His eyes immediately arrowed in on Ashleigh, standing in a row with three other bridesmaids. Out of the five beautiful women in the bridal party he saw only her—the smallest of them, luminous in a dusky pink dress, her bright hair pulled up off her face and entwined with creamy flowers. Her gaze was intent on the bride and groom. Even from where he stood, he could see the expressions flit across her face. Joy for her friends. Happiness. And a poignant longing that echoed how he felt as he gazed at her.

His longing was fierce, possessive. He wanted to see her dressed not as a bridesmaid but as a bride—*his* bride—with all that longing and joy lighting up her face for *him*. Now he had to convince her to trust him, to believe that he had left behind him any play-acting or pretence, and pray that she felt the same way he felt. He slid his hand in his breast pocket for the reassurance of that important piece of jewellery that he hoped would seal the most important deal of his life. And summoned up the courage to reveal his true self to her.

Lukas watched as the ceremony concluded. He had always prided himself on his lack of sentimentality. But when he watched the tall blonde bride and the dark-haired groom exchange a lingering kiss he felt overwhelmed by an agony of longing. *Yes.* This was what he wanted for him and Ashleigh.

He wanted to propose to her right now. But she was surrounded by people congratulating the happy couple. He considered himself a brave man. It had taken courage to make the difficult decisions required to save the family company. He was fearless in sport. But what if he asked Ashleigh to marry him in front of all these people and she said 'no'? Humiliation wasn't something he could wear lightly. He had to get her on her own, away from here.

'Ashleigh.' The voice was low and urgent. Did she want to be with Lukas so much she was conjuring up his voice at her shoulder? But no. Ashleigh turned to see him standing just behind her.

'You've gatecrashed my friends' wedding?' she hissed, while trying to deny the way her heart leapt at the sight of him. Tall and imposing in an immaculately tailored dark suit, he put the rest of the male guests to shame—including the incredibly handsome groom.

'I told the gatekeepers I was your significant other,' he said in a low voice.

'So we're back to the pretend now, are we?' she said through a sickening sense of disappointment. 'I thought that was what gave you such cause to doubt me? Maybe we should try sticking to the facts. You could have told them you were my boss and they would have let you in. Though the security is pretty tight. My friends have had a problem with paparazzi in the past.'

'I didn't realise you had friends in such high places,' he said. He seemed…nervous. Lukas Christophedes *nervous*? Surely he wouldn't be intimidated by the grand company here? Or was he intimidated by her less than friendly welcome?

She had no idea what he was doing here—not when he'd been so relieved to see the last of her that heartbreaking night of Tina's drinks. The night she had humiliated herself by revealing her feelings. Feelings he'd made so clear were not reciprocated. But if it went on past performance he must want something from her. Something related to his business—the work that meant more than anything to him. Certainly more than *she* could ever mean.

'You told me you weren't interested in weddings, so the titles of the bride and groom didn't come into it.'

'It's true I've never been interested in weddings. Though I could get interested if the circumstances were right.' Was he trying to tell her something? If so it was in some kind of male-speak code she had no idea how to decipher. But his tortured expression didn't give her any clues.

'That still doesn't explain why you're here,' she said. Hope leapt in her heart. Had he missed her? Come to ask her to come back? It had hurt, the way he'd let her go so easily, had seemed so relieved she'd decided to leave before Christmas.

He cleared his throat, took a step closer. She glanced over her shoulder. 'Try not to look too friendly,' she warned. 'And no need to act lovey-dovey—Tina's not here. However, Clio Caldwell is here and it's against Maids in Chelsea rules to fraternise with clients.' Not to mention push them against a wall and kiss them in a frenzy of want. Lukas was attracting a few interested looks. She had to be careful; she didn't want lose her job.

'I came to ask you…to ask you a favour,' he said finally.

Business again. Why had she thought it would be otherwise? She sighed. Hid her plummeting disappointment behind a matter-of-fact manner. 'What is it this time? And does it involve me requiring a complete change of wardrobe?'

'Just the clothes waiting for you back at home,' he said. *His* home, he meant. It could never be hers. Although, the way she felt about him, anywhere he was would be home. Why was he here, stirring up impossible feelings?

Ashleigh took a deep breath to steady herself. She really couldn't endure any more make-believe; it would be cruel of him to expect it of her. Not when she yearned for him to take her in his arms and tell her…oh, tell her impossible things like he'd fallen in love with her the way she'd fallen for him. That he wanted their relationship to be genuine. *Get real, Ashleigh*, she told herself. There was a far more likely explanation for his presence.

'Is Tina offering invitations again?' she asked. 'Maybe a double date with her and Gary that you think you can't refuse?' Unable to meet his gaze, she looked down at the floor, at a pattern in the carpet that seemed appropriately like a jagged red heart torn in two. 'If so, I think it might be time to tell her…to tell her you've crushed my heart and moved on.' Which wouldn't actually be far from the truth.

'It's not that.' There was a note of urgency to his voice that made her look up to find his dark brown eyes lit by something unfamiliar and unsettling as he searched her face.

'Then…then what is it?' she asked in a voice that came out shakier than she had meant it to. For a long moment her gaze met his and it seemed as though everything around her faded away—the chatting of the guests, the music, the happy laughter of the reunited bride and groom. She had the feeling that her world was about to change for ever.

'It…it's something personal. I… I want to ask

you to…to…' She wasn't used to seeing Lukas this uncertain, as if he were unable to get the words out.

'Ask me what, Lukas?' She clasped her hands behind her back so he wouldn't see they were trembling with nervous anticipation.

He took a deep, shuddering breath. 'Ashleigh, I…' he choked out.

'Yes?' she said.

One of the groom's friends, bearing two flutes of champagne, brushed past them, murmured an apology.

Lukas glared at him, then muttered something under his breath in Greek that didn't sound like a curse word, rather that he might be berating himself. Whatever it was, Ashleigh got the distinct impression he had changed his mind about what he was going to ask her—and that she might never know what it would have been.

She looked up at him, forced her voice to sound steady. 'Lukas, are you asking me to help you with something?'

He responded to her question as if to a lifeline. But his answer took her completely by surprise. 'Yes. My parents called to see when I'd be arriving in Athens for Christmas. When I told them I was spending Christmas in London they insisted on coming here to join me. They're arriving tomorrow morning, Christmas Eve.'

She frowned. 'And that involves me, how?'

'I want you to spend Christmas Day with me.'

Ashleigh was so astonished she was momentarily lost for words. 'So you want to hire me as your hostess?' she said eventually. *Work, after all.* 'If so, you need to talk to Clio.'

'No! I'm not saying that at all. I need someone there so I'm not outnumbered.'

Ashleigh almost choked on the nausea that rose in her throat. 'So you want to trundle out the pretend girlfriend again to make Christmas Day easier for you?' she managed to get out, aware she needed to keep her voice low so interested bystanders couldn't hear her. 'Well, I don't even have to think about it. I've paid over and over for my mistake in squatting in your house. The ledger is balanced; as a matter of fact, there's probably credit in my column. My answer is *no*. The deal is *off.*' They were equals here. Ashleigh and Lukas. Not the billionaire and his errant maid. In fact *he* was the intruder into *her* world.

He paled beneath his tan and she could see a pulse throb at the corner of his mouth. 'You couldn't be more wrong. I need someone to give me moral support. Watch my back. I want someone to be on my side.'

'And that's me?'

She saw a new vulnerability in his eyes, an appeal. 'Right now, Ashleigh, I can't think of anyone more on my side than you.' He looked and sounded so sincere—but then he'd proven himself to be a top-notch actor.

'Really?'

'Yes. I… I need you. Not for business reasons. This is…this is personal.'

He *needed* her. The word flashed out a warning that if she went along with this she was heading into danger. Danger to her heart, danger to her sanity. Because the thought of him needing her was alluring beyond reason. She wasn't at all sure what this was about. It was far from the declaration of devotion that would have sent her heart singing. But she had missed him. There wasn't a minute since they'd parted that she hadn't missed him.

He needed her.

Spending Christmas Day with him would be a cruel torture. How could she endure having to fall back into the easy repartee, the flirtatious fake kisses, the pretence of being someone special to him when she ached for it to be real? When it could never be real. Why had she let herself fall in love with such an unattainable, difficult, *damaged* man? A man who had given no indication he reciprocated her feelings. He had admitted he was attracted to her. But that wasn't enough. Her heart would be breaking knowing that once her usefulness had expired, his parents back on a flight to Athens, it would be *goodbye, Ashleigh*.

And yet… He needed her. She kept coming back to that. No matter what his motivation for having her back in his house, she wanted to be with him. And it would be a milder form of torture than if she was without him. If she said 'no' to his proposition, she would most likely spend the most miserable Christmas Day of her life wondering what he was doing.

Sadly, it seemed he thought he could just pick her up and put her down again as he chose. But if she went into this with her eyes open, knowing the likely consequences, knowing it would be for the last time, she would say yes. For his sake, but also for her own.

'I actually have plans for Christmas Day,' she said.

'Surely you could change them,' he said, with the arrogant assurance of a man used to getting his own way.

'I'll have to talk to Sophie.' In between their bridesmaid preparations, she had taken her friend into her confidence about her feelings for Lukas. Sophie wouldn't think she was blowing her off for a better offer if she accepted Lukas's invitation. But it would be good manners to check first.

'Of course,' he said. He waited, obviously impatient if the tapping of his foot had anything to do with it, while she went to look for Sophie. She found her with Grace, who had seemed subdued all through the renewal ceremony. The friends all knew it was Grace's first Christmas on her own since her beloved grandmother had died. Ashleigh joined Sophie in giving her a big hug and suggesting they catch up over Christmas.

'All okay,' she said to Lukas when she got back. 'I'll be there.'

'Please convey my thanks to Sophie,' he said

in a formal way that made her smile. But there was gratitude underscoring his words.

'Shall do,' she said. 'You know I'm needed here on bridesmaid duty and will be staying at the hotel with the others tonight?'

'As long as you are with me on Christmas Day.'

She still wasn't sure what this was all about but she looked up at him, willed him to believe her. 'Now I've committed to this, I won't let you down, Lukas. You can trust me.'

He placed his hand on her cheek, gently, tenderly, and she didn't care if Clio saw it. 'I'm beginning to believe that,' he said.

'Good,' she said, placing her hand over his. Was this a subtle change in direction for them? If so, she realised they would have to take it step by step. Or was it just him manipulating her for his own ends?

But, in spite of her confusion, there were practical considerations surrounding Christmas Day in Chelsea. 'What about Christmas dinner?' she said. 'You say you're good at making toast, Lukas, but how are you going to handle a meal for four people?'

'All sorted. Everything is coming from Harrods. It's being delivered tomorrow.'

'How the other half lives,' she said with a sigh. 'They say the rich are different.'

'I'm not so different, am I?' he said.

'You're actually quite nice,' she said with a grudging smile. *Back to the mock flirtation.*

'Quite nice? I think I'll take that as a compliment,' he said, returning her smile and holding her gaze with his own.

'Please do,' she said.

For one long moment she thought he was going to kiss her, there in the middle of the wedding party with all eyes on them. Instead he took both her hands in his and drew her closer in a gesture that seemed almost as intimate. 'Thank you,' he said. She felt he was thanking her for so much more than a compliment—but she wasn't sure what it was.

'Just one thing—how will you introduce me to your parents?' she said. 'As your maid?'

'As my friend,' he said. 'Maybe we can work up from there.'

Which didn't actually make his intentions any clearer.

CHAPTER FOURTEEN

WHEN THE DOORBELL rang at noon on Christmas Eve, Lukas thought it was a delivery from Harrods. But it wasn't.

Ashleigh stood on the threshold. 'I know you said Christmas Day but I thought I could make myself useful on Christmas Eve,' she said. 'Is that okay?'

Her smile was tentative as she looked up at him, fresh faced, her cheeks pink from the cold, the pale winter sunlight dancing off her hair in sparks of gold. She was wearing jeans and the dreaded anorak and she had never looked lovelier. On first impression, he had thought Ashleigh to be wholesome and unsophisticated. She had proved to be so much more complex than that.

'More than okay,' he said.

Much to his mortification, he hadn't been able to get out the words he'd wanted to at the wedding party. It wasn't that he'd been scared to propose for the first time in his life—of course he hadn't—it had been too public for something so momentous and private. Now she was here and he would have another chance when the time was right.

He wanted no more pretence, no more lies— no matter how well intentioned—no more hiding behind his workaholic barrier. So he followed his first impulse. 'Come on in,' he said. 'I'm so glad you're here.' Then he pulled her to him in a hug. He tightened his arms around her and closed his eyes in sheer joy and gratitude that she had come back to him. She stiffened against him at first, then relaxed into his embrace.

'You have your backpack,' he said, pointing out the obvious as he'd actually hugged that too.

'Yes,' she said. 'I'm calling in the offer of accommodation until after Christmas. Sophie's sofa will be there for me after that.'

'Your room is waiting for you,' he said. If he had his way she would never sleep on her friend's sofa again. Or indeed that bed in the guest room.

'Are your parents here?' she said, peering around him into the hallway.

'I sent them off in the car for some last-minute

shopping. My mother loves Peter Jones in Sloane Square.'

'I seriously am here to help,' she said, slipping off her anorak to reveal the long-sleeved black T-shirt. He couldn't help checking for trainers—the huge hate of his mother's. Even though his parents exasperated him, he wanted Ashleigh to make a good impression. *As herself.* But trainers would get her off to the wrong start. Thankfully, he saw neat ankle-length black boots. The kind of shoes his mother would approve of being worn in the house.

Ashleigh had followed the direction of his glance. 'The sales have started,' she said by way of explanation.

'My mother will be in heaven,' he said.

'Not when she has to elbow her way through the crowds, she won't,' said Ashleigh with a flash of dimples.

'I appreciate your offer of help,' he said. 'But you're not here as a maid, you know. You're a guest.'

'What kind of a friend would I be if I didn't check to see if all is okay?'

'When you actually were the maid you did such a good job everything is in perfect order.'

'Fresh towels and toiletries in the bathrooms?'

'I guess so.'

'But do you *know* so?'

'Not something I would think to check.'

'So I'll do the checking. And all the other stuff you mightn't have thought of because you're used to having staff.' It wasn't a criticism; she was smiling at him. 'It's a routine I got used to here.'

'Thank you,' he said. 'I'll take your backpack up to your room.'

'Great,' she said, already turning away to head towards her self-imposed chores.

He paused. 'Ashleigh, wait,' he said.

She turned back, her hair swishing around her shoulders. He wanted to run his hands through it, tilt her face up for his kiss. But there would be time for that if all went to plan. 'Yes?' she said.

'The clothes in your room. They're all yours, you know. To wear them, to give them away, to sell them, whatever you wish to do with them.'

'I... I can't think of them as mine. They belong to the pretend girlfriend. The wardrobe you bought for her to play her role as your fake date.'

'Didn't you say every Ashleigh I saw was a facet of you?'

'Yes,' she said, eyes downcast.

'Doesn't that glamorous Ashleigh like those clothes?' he said quietly.

'She loves them, of course she does. But they don't belong to her. I would be wearing them under false pretences.'

He placed his fingers under her chin to tilt her face towards his. 'You should wear them. Please. I'll throw the lot out if you don't.'

'I'm sure a charity would welcome them.'

There wasn't a gold-digging bone in her body. She still hadn't figured out that the worth of the watch, if sold, would buy her a considerable number of nights in one of those West End hotels he had 'billed' her for. But he didn't intend she'd be sleeping anywhere but under his roof. Ever.

'You might need to wear them while my parents are here.'

'You're right,' she said. 'For one last spin of the pretend girlfriend.' She put up her hand to block his protest. 'Because if your parents are anything like my parents, they will immediately look for a relationship whether or not one exists.'

Now. He should say something now. But his pause lost him his chance.

Ashleigh continued. 'I would make a better impression for you in designer clothes.'

'True—when you meet my mother you'll see just how true,' he said. 'But you look perfectly fine in what you're wearing. I… I like whichever facet of Ashleigh I see.'

'Even anorak Ashleigh?' she said with, at last, a teasing glimpse of dimples.

'Maybe not that Ashleigh,' he conceded. 'Though it's the anorak, not the Ashleigh I object to. It's not warm enough either. Snow is predicted. Would you please keep the warm coat?'

She hesitated. He could see the indecision ripple over her features. 'Okay. Thank you. I'll keep the coat.'

'And the anorak?'

'It shall be burned, thrown on the Yule log and consigned to the flames,' she said dramatically though her voice wasn't steady. He realised what an effort it was for her to keep up the façade. His indecision was hurting her. 'Though I'd better check first with my sister, who owns it.'

'You do that,' he said. *She was adorable.* She

turned away again. 'One more thing before you go,' he said. 'Thank you for my gift, the beautiful pomegranate ornament.'

She flushed high on her cheekbones. 'You found it. I'm so glad you like it.'

'I will treasure it,' he said. 'It's too fragile to hang over the front door. Perhaps you could help me hang it on that amazing tree you set up in the living room?'

'I… I would love that,' she said, looking up at him.

Then Lukas realised she was standing right under the mistletoe she had hung from the chandelier above them. He saw an invitation to a kiss in the gleam of her blue eyes, the slight parting of her lush lips. This couldn't wait.

He dipped his head to claim her mouth. She responded immediately and wound her arms around his neck to bring him closer, to press her body close to his. She made a little murmur of pleasure deep in her throat. With an answering groan he deepened the kiss. He wanted to hear more: whimpers of need, sighs of pleasure, moans of ecstasy from this wonderful, perfect woman. *His woman.* He slid his hands down her back, her waist, to come to rest cupping the curves of her bottom.

That, of course, had to be the moment his parents burst through the front door, laden with parcels and complaining about the London traffic.

Ashleigh dropped her arms from around Lukas's neck, felt the hot tide of a furious blush colour her cheeks.

The older couple froze. It would almost be comical if she didn't feel so mortified. She had hoped to meet Lukas's parents under more dignified circumstances than this. Although this was certainly more dignified than the way she'd met their son.

Lukas stepped forward. 'Mother,' he said, indicating the beautifully groomed woman looking at her in wide-eyed astonishment. 'Father,' Lukas said, indicating the broad-shouldered man with iron-grey curly hair and thick black eyebrows. 'This is Ashleigh,' he said, indicating her.

Ashleigh stepped forward. 'Hello, Mr and Mrs Christophedes. Er... Merry Christmas.' What had that kiss been about? It had seemed real. Fired by genuine passion. By—dare she hope?—

genuine *feeling*. This was getting more confusing by the second.

'Ashleigh is the…the friend I told you about who will be staying with us for Christmas,' said Lukas. 'She has arrived early.'

'To help,' she jumped in. 'I've come early to give Lukas a hand with the Christmas dinner and…and anything else he might need.'

That didn't sound right. Not when he'd had a possessive hold of her bottom. So much for the *friends* theory. The parents would be as unsure as she herself was about how she fitted in to Lukas's life.

His mother had the same deep brown eyes as Lukas and they gleamed with curiosity. She offloaded her parcels onto her already overburdened husband and made a beeline for Ashleigh.

She held out a perfectly manicured hand for Ashleigh to shake. 'I am Efthalia—my friends call me Effie. I hope that is what you will call me.'

Ashleigh returned the older woman's handshake. 'Thank you, Effie. It's a pleasure to meet you.'

'My husband is Dimitris,' she said, indicating Lukas's parcel-laden father.

The man shrugged to indicate his inability to free his hands from the multitude of parcels so he could shake hands. Instead he nodded. 'Hello, Ashleigh,' he said, with a warm smile and a glance to his son.

It wasn't just his mother who was curious. *What had she got herself into?* A new game called by Lukas, of which she was uncertain of the rules.

'Can I help you with those parcels?' she asked. 'You've done a lot of Christmas shopping.'

'Most of it is for her,' Dimitris said, indicating his wife with a raising of his dark brows.

'Why else would I come to London except to shop?' Effie said blithely. Then she turned to Lukas. 'And to see my beloved son for Christmas,' she said, her voice breaking.

'He's thrilled that you're here,' said Ashleigh diplomatically, sensing the sincerity—and pain—in his mother's voice.

Lukas took some of the shopping bags and parcels from his father. Effie was wearing a superb red coat. Ashleigh recognised it as the same label as the leopard print coat, as her lavender ball gown. She could see why Lukas saw a resemblance to his mother in Tina. Effie had the same cleverly tinted blonde hair, the same look of a very well maintained older woman. But she was more beautiful. And there was a depth of pain and remorse in her eyes when she looked at her son.

'Where do you want these put, Mother?' Lukas asked.

'Some to my room, others I need to gift wrap.'

'May I suggest the kitchen table for a gift-wrapping station?' Ashleigh said. 'Let me take some parcels down for you.'

Lukas shot her a grateful look.

'While I'm there, I can make tea or coffee,' she added. 'I'll bring it upstairs here to serve.'

'I can drink tea in the kitchen,' said Effie. 'I will come with you.'

Ashleigh suspected she would be subjected to a vigorous grilling about her relationship with her son. She decided to stick to the truth as closely as possible.

Later that day, in the dimming light of late afternoon, she walked up Sloane Street with Lukas, heading for Knightsbridge. The chauffeur had dropped them when she'd suggested it would be quicker to walk than drive in the practically stalled Christmas Eve traffic.

Lukas had said he had some last-minute shopping to do at Harrods for provisions and had *insisted* she go with him. She hadn't needed much convincing. The situation had become so awkward she'd welcomed the chance to escape the house. And to be alone with him. They'd left his parents bickering over their gift-wrapping in the kitchen.

Now she would have a chance to call him on the way this day was panning out. What his invitation to share Christmas with him really meant. But she had to pick her moment.

'I like your parents,' she said. 'I didn't expect to, after what you've told me about them, but I did. They're charming and warm and good company.'

Lukas's mouth twisted. 'They're the kind of people you'd like to chat with at a party rather than have parent you.'

'Maybe they didn't know how to parent. That's why they made such a mess of it. But they love you. There can be no doubt about that. Now your welfare is of utmost concern to them. Maybe… maybe they've grown up too.'

'I know,' he said. 'That's why I let them come for Christmas.'

'They're desperate for grandchildren.'

He cursed under his breath. 'My mother didn't harass you about that, did she? She saw through the "friends" thing straight away.'

'Considering how she caught us kissing, that shouldn't surprise you. I didn't deny we were more than friends.'

'What did you tell her?' he said. 'So we keep our stories straight.'

More play-acting and pretence. She was over it. Lukas either let her in on the new game or she was off to Sophie's flat the moment dinner was over. Her friend had given her the spare key, just in case. And she hadn't unpacked her backpack.

'I told her the truth—well, nearly the truth. That I'd run away from my wedding in Australia. That I was working for Maids in Chelsea until I found a position as an accountant, and got a job as a live-in maid in your house. That's how we met. I did not mention the bathtub.'

'Good,' he said. 'That most memorable of meetings will stay strictly between us.'

'Talking about memorable, what was that kiss back there all about?' she said.

'You seemed to enjoy it,' he said evasively.

'Of course I enjoyed it. It was a wonderful kiss. It felt like a *real* kiss. Was it real, Lukas?'

He cleared his throat. 'This is hardly the time and the place for a discussion like that.'

'When *will* be the time and the place for it?' she said. 'Because I'm confused. And I'm getting cranky about being confused.'

'After we get to Harrods. It closes at five so we need to rush.'

She stopped in the middle of the pavement and let the Christmas shopping hordes of humanity pass by her. 'Seriously, Lukas. You'd better have some explanations for me. Not only for my sake. But to make it easier for me to talk to your parents without making an utter fool of myself.'

'You will get an explanation,' he said. 'Come on. We have to keep moving.'

She had to quicken her pace to keep up with him. 'I'll hold you to that. Your mother told me

I was the first "female friend" you've introduced them to for many years.'

'That's true. I didn't consider my private life any of their business. Be wary of what you say to them.'

'For what it's worth, I think they'd be wonderful grandparents. Perhaps they want to try and get it right the second time around.'

'Humph,' said Lukas in typical manner. No doubt warning her that she was not in the running as consideration as the mother of the grandbabies. Did he realise how hurtful he was being?

They neared the top of Sloane Street and Ashleigh stopped to admire the Christmas lights. 'I can't wait to see Harrods all lit up and—'

She paused as she felt something cold and damp drift onto her cheek. Then looked up to see a flurry of snowflakes cascading towards her. 'Lukas. It's snowing. It's snowing for Christmas! I can't tell you how exciting this is for an Aussie girl.'

She did a little jig of joy on the pavement. People walking by them laughed, but in a good-natured way—a spirit-of-the-season way.

Lukas picked her up and whirled her around.

'You are enchanting, Ashleigh Murphy. Has any-one ever told you that before?'

She thrilled to the light in his eyes. *What was this about?* 'Actually, they haven't.' Something about him was very, very different. Something exciting. Something she could not bring herself to believe. Again she felt that sensation of im-pending change.

'I'm telling you now. Ashleigh, that kiss was real. I kissed you without any pretence. As me, Lukas, kissing you, Ashleigh.'

She caught her breath. 'Are you feeling it, Lukas?'

'I'm feeling it,' he said. 'Thanks to you, you beautiful woman.' And he picked up her hand and placed it on his chest, just like she had done to him the other night. She couldn't feel a thing through his overcoat except a wall of muscle. But she felt the pulsing of something strong and per-fect and life-changing in her heart.

'I wasn't going to tell you this. But your mother asked me was I in love with you,' she said.

His dark eyebrows rose. 'And what did you say?' Again, she sensed his vulnerability, that he needed answers from her as much as she did from him.

This was no time for pretence on her part either. 'I… I told her the truth.'

'And that was…?' She got the distinct impression he was holding his breath for her reply.

'That I was head-over-heels in love with you.' She reached up and pulled his head to hers, looked up into his eyes. 'I love you, Lukas.'

He looked down into her face with relief, joy, and something else so wonderful and exciting her heart started a furious beating. He let out his breath on words she had never imagined she would hear. 'I love you too, *agápi mou.*'

His voice sounded rusty, as though he hadn't said those words for a very long time. Or maybe it was because he was finally letting himself feel the emotions he had blocked for so long.

He kissed her, long and sweet and tenderly, to the sound of cheers and clapping from the circle of well-wishers who had formed around them.

Ashleigh broke away from the kiss, looked around her and grinned at the expressions of goodwill on all the different cosmopolitan faces around them. It was only then that she realised they were standing in each other's arms in front of the most famous jewellery shop in the world. Tiffany. Fingers of excitement marched up her spine. Were they in this particular spot by accident or by Lukas's design?

She looked up to him for an answer.

'We didn't get it clear the other night about what you actually felt about commitment, about marriage, about children,' he said. 'Is it what you want?'

She had to clear her suddenly choked-up throat to reply. She forgot they had an avid audience hanging onto their every word. 'With the right person. Yes.'

'I never wanted all that before. In fact I've run from it. But I want it now. With you, Ashleigh. Will you marry me?'

Dan had hounded her for years to get her to agree to marry him. With Lukas it took all of two seconds. 'Yes, Lukas, yes,' she said. 'I will marry you.'

His smile was wide with relief and happiness and he had never looked more handsome, with snowflakes frosting his dark hair. He took a small velvet box in a distinctive pale blue from his pocket. Then flipped it open to reveal a huge diamond, simply and elegantly set on a platinum band. 'What do you think?' he asked. 'If you don't like it we can go inside and choose another more to your—'

She stopped him with a swift kiss. 'It's perfect,' she breathed. 'I love it.' He picked up her left hand and slipped the ring on her third finger, where it sparkled in the glow of the Christmas lights that twinkled all around them. 'And I love you more than I can say.'

Lukas kissed her again. The man who would be her husband kissed her long and slow and thoroughly and she, his wife-to-be, kissed him back with all her heart as the snow drifted down on their heads and the Christmas shoppers of London cheered their approval and delight.

CHAPTER FIFTEEN

AT CHRISTMAS TIME Australia was nearly a day ahead of London. It was already Christmas morning there as Ashleigh prepared to video-call her family in Bundaberg. She would have left it at a phone call if Dan had been there—anything else would have been most inappropriate. But, thankfully, he had decided to join his father at the Gold Coast.

Ashleigh sat alone behind Lukas's desk in front of his large-screen computer and keyed in the family code. When the screen came to life, her family were grouped on the sofa, her father in shorts, her mother and sister in brightly coloured sundresses. Her sister's husband was there too and her aunt and uncle. Yes, her mother was wearing her glittery antler-shaped earrings that played *Rudolph the Red-Nosed Reindeer* at random intervals. Ashleigh prayed they were switched off.

'Merry Christmas,' she said through sudden tears she had to choke back.

'Merry Christmas,' her family chorused as they all waved. Her sister picked up the family tabby cat from a cushion beside her and made him wave a paw too.

'Are you okay, sweetie?' her mother said. 'That doesn't look like Sophie's parents' house behind you. It looks like a library. You're not on your own, are you? Not lonely? Not cold?'

Ashleigh laughed. 'It's a study, Mum. And I'm not alone.' She beckoned to Lukas, who was standing out of range of the camera with Effie and Dimitris, to join her. Ashleigh shifted in her chair to make room for him beside her. He brought his head to the same level as hers, his cheek against hers. She looked into his face and smiled her love and happiness. The expression on her family's faces was priceless.

'This is Lukas Christophedes,' she said.

'Merry Christmas,' said Lukas with a big smile and his slight Greek accent.

Her mother was obviously too stunned to say anything but her sister jumped in with a tentative 'Hi, Lukas.'

Her father was more forthcoming. 'And who is Lukas Christophedes when he's at home?' he growled.

'He's the man I'm spending Christmas Day with,' Ashleigh said. 'And the man I'm going to spend the rest of my life with.'

Then she splayed her left hand with the beautiful diamond ring on her third finger in front of the computer's camera so it filled her family's screen.

When all the excited squeals and expressions of disbelief had died away she spoke again. 'Mum. Dad. Everyone. I know you all love Dan. But I didn't. Not enough to marry, anyway. I love Lukas more than I could ever have imagined I could love a person. This is real, this is for ever. I want you to accept him into the family.'

Her family all looked at each other and then back at the camera. Her mother was the first to speak. 'Whatever makes you happy, sweetie. Congratulations. Welcome, Lukas.'

'Thank you,' he said.

'There's a couple of other people I want you to welcome too,' Ashleigh said. She beckoned Effie and Dimitris to the camera and introduced them as her future parents-in-law.

'So when will the wedding take place?' asked her mother.

'In summer. I don't see myself as a winter bride,' Ashleigh said. 'We'll get married in London.' She wanted to make that clear from the start.

Dimitris beamed expansively. 'Of course Lukas will fly you all over for the wedding. Then for a big party on our family's private island in Greece.'

That caused a flurry of excited reactions. Her father glared at the camera. 'We'll pay our own way to London for our daughter's wedding, thank you very much.'

Her mother jabbed him in the ribs with her elbow. 'And to the private Greek island, don't forget that.'

Lukas put up his hand. 'I understand that you are concerned you do not know me. And that this has all happened very quickly. But I can assure you I love Ashleigh and will look after her and cherish her for the rest of her life.'

'While letting me be my own person at the same time,' Ashleigh added.

'We are also planning to come and visit you in the new year,' Lukas said. 'That is, if it meets with your approval.'

Lukas turned to her and smiled. She smiled back and hoped her family could see the intensity of her joy. Perhaps they did. Because when he kissed her it was to a chorus of approval and applause from the other side of the world.

* * * * *